PRAISE FOR THE SILVER MYSTERY SERIES

"The main characters are compelling. Foiled Silver has everything: humor, mystery, even a little romance. You keep reading as the excitement builds to a smashing and surprising conclusion!"

—Dana Newman, Executive Director,
Talbot County Free Library

"Susan Reiss captures the magic, mystery and charm of that quintessential Eastern Shore town – St. Michaels. Secrets lay hidden for generations among the stunningly beautiful estates along the Miles River. Can't wait for her next 'silver' adventure."

—Kathy Harig, Proprietor,
Mystery Loves Company Bookstore

"*Tarnished Silver* is a fabulous debut novel! Abby Strickland is someone I can relate to, my kind of heroine. I admire the way she rises to the challenges thrown in her path. She's a brave and loyal person whom I would love to call a friend (if she were real, of course). Susan Reiss is a great storyteller, and I'm really looking forward to more stories in the Silver Mystery Series.

—Kassandra Lamb, author,
Kate Huntington Mystery Series

"Silver, art and murder lead to an exciting read!"

—S. Jennifer Sugarman, artist

"This series will transport you to the Eastern Shore of Maryland, but will remind you of whatever town has a special place in your heart—hopefully without murder. It leaves me wondering what other secrets this quaint little Eastern Shore town is hiding and I'm waiting for Susan Reiss to tell us."

—Barbara Viniar, Retired President
Chesapeake College, Wye Mills, Maryland

"This is a series that captures the local flavor of our area – St. Michaels, the food and the quirky characters who live here and visit. The descriptions of all the real places make me feel like I'm there. The mystery kept me turning the page. This is a series I recommend to my library patrons… and to you.

—Shauna Beulah, Branch Manager,
St. Michaels Library

SILVER MYSTERY SERIES BOOKS

Tarnished Silver
Sacred Silver
Painted Silver
Hammered Silver
Foiled Silver
Deathly Silverr

DEATHLY SILVER

SUSAN REISS

Ink & Imagination

INK & IMAGINATION PRESS
an imprint of Blue Lily Publishers

This is a work of fiction.
Any resemblance to a person, living or dead, is unintentional and accidental.

Author Photo by Marie Martin

ISBN 978-1-949876-37-6 (e-book)
ISBN 978-1-949876-35-2 (print)

Website: www.SusanReiss.com
Facebook: Susan Reiss
Twitter: @Susan Reiss
Goodreads.com: Susan Reiss, Goodreads Author

To Ken and Pat

*for all your help and support and hours of driving
while we developed the characters*

CHAPTER ONE

A finely prepared dinner deserves the compliment of being served with the appropriate and correct silver serving pieces. It showcases the various dishes and honors the efforts of the staff.

> "The Butler's Guide to Fine Silver"
> Mr. Hollister 1898

In the candlelit dining room, our hostess Kitty sat calmly at the table with her guests. Suddenly, she jumped out of her chair, her snow-white curls dancing wildly. Her piercing scream shattered the quiet conversations going on around the table. She pointed out the window at a black cloaked figure on the lawn. Mesmerized, we stared at the figure pointing back at us.

Then there was a clatter and thud. Kitty fainted dead away, taking her chair and some of the china, crystal goblets and silver with her to the floor. The spell broken, we jumped into action to revive Kitty, stop the flow of wine and water across the tablecloth to the oriental rug below and reposition the roast on its platter.

When I glanced around, I realized that the men had raced out of the room to nab the prankster… or was it a ghost?

Looking back to the beginning of the evening, what happened wasn't what I'd expected. he, that is. Up until the moment of the scream and the drama that followed, the dinner party had been perfect… good food, good conversation…all that I'd hoped my dear friend Lorraine would enjoy. I'd thought it was what she needed after the trauma we'd experienced. It hadn't been that long since the murder of her closest friend Evelyn and the discovery of her killer. Had I forced her to accept this dinner invitation before she was ready to rejoin the usual flow of life on the Eastern Shore of the Chesapeake Bay?

Earlier, she'd looked calm, though a little subdued, as we moved to Kitty's elegant dining room. The table was set with lovely china, crystal and, of course, shimmering sterling silver. People always pulled out their silver when they invited Lorraine, because she was known for her vast collection of flatware—knives, forks, spoons—and valuable silver pieces, like tea sets, bowls, pea spoons and the impressive epergne used as a centerpiece. It wasn't unusual for a hostess or her husband to pull me aside at some point during the evening to ask how much a particular piece might be worth. I was known as Lorraine's in-house silver appraiser of her vast silver collection. We didn't have a long history, but it was deep and complicated.

When Kitty's guests had moved into the dining room, my attention was drawn first to the formal, but spooky table setting: a black satin tablecloth and pumpkin orange tapers in silver candlesticks. I felt like I was attending a kid's Halloween party, for goodness sake. Maybe accepting this invitation wasn't such a good idea. I sighed and looked out the large palladium window and the spectacular view of the lawn and woods, the natural beauty of the Shore. Oak and maple trees had almost reached their height of fall color and the local crepe myrtles were holding on to the last of their fuchsia and pink blooms.

Kitty's slow Southern drawl pulled my attention back into the room. "Abby, your place is next to Robert."

I moved to sit down and wondered what I'd have to say to Robert Chamberlain, heir of the Chamberlain Companies. He had walked away from his family's conglomerate and started his own company to compete with his sister who, after a last-minute change in their father's will, had inherited all the Chamberlain companies.

No one could accuse Kitty of being subtle. Robert was single, but he wasn't the only one at the table. There was Dr. Greene, fresh from giving a speech at a medical gathering at the Ocean City Convention Center only an hour away, but he was older, closer to Lorraine's age. Kitty probably thought the good doctor was much too old for me, a woman nearing her thirtieth birthday.

I stole a look at Lorraine and noticed that the doctor had caught her eye. That little flicker of interest made me smile. He was just the kind of man who would attract her—well-educated, handsome and well-dressed.

A little glint at the cuff of his sleeve snagged my attention. "Oh, are you wearing cufflinks, Doctor?" I asked. "I thought men didn't bothered with them anymore."

He pulled his cuff to reveal a silver cufflink with a small symbol on it. "I take them out whenever I go to a medical conference." He gave me a wry smile. "My father gave them to me when I graduated from medical school. Unfortunately, he's no longer with us." He held his arm so the cufflink could be admired.

"And the symbol etched there is a caduceus?" I asked.

"Yes, it reminds me of the man who inspired me to become a doctor."

"I've always wondered why a snake is part of that symbol. Do you know?"

"I think it symbolizes rejuvenation and hope for a speedy recovery, because a snake sheds its skin to start a new phase of its life."

Other guests were meandering into the dining room and took their seats. An older man with sharp, military posture escorted his wife, Audrey, whose flamboyant red hair matched her personality. My friend Lisa, a petite blonde, came in wearing a fire engine red dress and bolero jacket.

"Lisa, what a great look," I said. It was a sincere compliment, though I was a little surprised to see such a feminine look worn by a successful chef who ran her kitchen with an iron fist. I loved the color, but I could never wear it with my deep auburn curls cascading below my shoulders.

"Oh, thanks, Abby. I always wear white when I'm working, but never outside the kitchen. It's nice to get out and wear a bright color for a change," she explained and moved to find her seat.

Such intense people always baffled me. Some fizzled out early in their careers like a firework dud. For others, I supposed their intensity was their key to success. Still, life could force changes. I wondered if Lisa would wear white if she ever got married in a traditional ceremony.

Lorraine walked into the dining room and smiled her approval. "Oh, Kitty, what a lovely table! So unique and appropriate for the evening." She was referring to the rather unusual table setting.

"Oh! Do you like it? I'm thrilled!" Kitty giggled. "I know it's a rather unorthodox setting, but I just love how the black makes the silver stand out." She put her hand on her husband Harold's arm. "And I thought it was incredibly appropriate for tonight's dinner theme."

Harold explained. "As we said when we invited you all, I thought this would be an excellent time to enlist your help. I don't know why, but my lovely wife Kitty gets so frightened by the silly superstitions that come out at Halloween and things that go bump in the night that she has nightmares from now until Thanksgiving. I've tried everything. I hope you've all brought a scary story with you. Maybe surrounded by friends, she'll get over her fears."

That explained the spooky black linens. It made sense with

Halloween only a few days away. I hoped Kitty wasn't going to suggest a séance with dessert.

"Oh, Harold dear, you make me sound like such a ninny." She turned to all of us and winked. "I think he was looking for an excuse to have a dinner party!"

"No, Kitty, I'm just trying find a way to get some sleep in the next few weeks. Can't have you shouting out in the middle of the night anymore."

While people, especially the women, made comforting noises, I noticed that Lorraine was scanning the table and the guests. A slight frown crossed her forehead. "Kitty, am I counting right?"

The other guests looked lost, and I had to admit it took me a moment to figure out what she meant.

"I know," Kitty said with a solemn face. "There are nine people. I do hate an unbalanced table."

"Unbalanced?" Robert asked.

"Yes, an extra man or woman," I explained. "A hostess strives for an even number of guests."

Audrey, Carl's flashy wife, chimed in. "Where's Gretchen? Why didn't you invite her? She could have balanced the boat, so to speak."

"I wanted to invite her, but I couldn't find an eligible man in time for the party. Then when Dr. Greene let me know he was going to be on the Shore for a meeting, I extended the invitation to him to come. I reached out to Gretchen, but she said she couldn't come. She had other plans. I was rather surprised because she's always willing... eager to accept our invitations. I love hearing the latest from the comic book world and seeing her drawings. She is such a gifted cartoonist. But it wasn't meant to be this time. She said she had other plans."

Lisa, the chef who probably knew a lot about entertaining guidelines and maxims, piped up. "You know, Kitty, they say an unbalanced table is bad luck."

"I know, I know." Kitty moaned. "I tried to fix it, but life wouldn't cooperate. We just have to keep our fingers crossed that everything will be alright."

"Please remember, my dear, the purpose of this dinner is to dispel superstitions, not feed them." Harold chuckled. "Remember, I need my beauty sleep."

Everyone laughed and a cheerful atmosphere was restored. With napkins in place and a toast to our hosts, we settled in to enjoy our Blue crab cocktail.

"I find it amazing how crab always tastes so much better on the Eastern Shore," Dr. Greene said between bites.

"It's all in how it's caught," Lorraine said with a wink. "I'll have to tell you a story sometime about catching… actually, it's called *pulling* crabs."

"Lorraine," Harold said, as if inspired. "You were raised here. Why don't you get us started by telling us a scary story of the Eastern Shore?"

I almost came out of my chair. Didn't the man remember the murder that happened at Fair Winds, Lorraine's home? I started to say something, but Lorraine waved me off and launched into the topic.

"There are lots of stories about hauntings all around the Maryland Eastern Shore. We have a rather robust ghost tour and cemetery crawl industry here in Talbot County."

Audrey flipped her red hair. "Do you know any stories about witches?" she asked.

Lorraine shook her head slowly. "No, I think you have to go to New England for that."

Audrey pursed her bright red lips and looked away, disappointed.

Lorraine cocked her head, thinking. "As I remember, there are a couple of stories about two women who were believed to be witches, but I think they were just old and crotchety." She flashed Audrey a smile. "We do have a lot of ghosts, even Robert E. Lee. He likes to haunt a hotel in the middle of St. Michaels where he once spent one or two nights." The group perked up. "I do have a story that is quite scary and rumored to be true."

We all sat up a little straighter, ready to listen, ready to be frightened. And she began. "I first heard the story when I was about eight years old and it still gives me the shivers."

At that moment, Kitty's cook brought in the standing rib roast on a platter complete with a matching silver carving set and placed it in front of Harold. Everyone applauded. But the silver knife would never touch the roast beef.

As Harold stood to carve the roast, Kitty let out a scream that should have shattered the crystal glasses on the table. She jumped up, turning over her chair with a clatter. Tears sprang to her eyes. She screamed again as she raised a trembling hand and pointed through the dining room window.

Outside, a figure in a long black cloak stood at the edge of the woods, its arm extended and a finger pointing straight at us.

The Grim Reaper.

Had he come to claim a soul?

CHAPTER TWO

There are two sizes of carving sets. The determination of which is appropriate to use is based on the meat entrée.

"The Butler's Guide to Fine Silver"
Mr. Hollister, 1898

The men jumped to their feet and dashed out of the room with Harold brandishing the carving knife. I was tempted to follow them, but Lorraine held up her hand to hold me back. "Let them handle it, Abby. It's not our problem."

Lorraine and Lisa went to Kitty to calm her.

Audrey sprang up from her chair. "I know what we need. Brandy!" And she raced out of the room.

I walked over to the large window and looked out on the lawn, but the Grim Reaper was gone. I caught glimpses of the men dashing around, trying to find the black-hooded figure. The blues, greens and grays of their clothing tended to blend into the woodsy background so it was difficult to follow their progress. Everything was dusky, except for the touch of red. Red? The only person wearing red was a woman. Lisa.

I spun my head around to check out the people helping Kitty. Lisa wasn't there. Had she gone out to join the search? I stifled the urge to join her. There was no reason to add to the chaos by upsetting Lorraine. So, I stood at the window and waited so quietly that I jumped when the kitchen door slammed and Robert rushed into the room.

"She's dead! She's dead!" he announced.

"Who's dead?" But my thoughts went to Lisa immediately.

Robert was gasping for breath, either from his run back to the house or from overwhelming emotions of shock and terror. "The Grim Reaper."

"Don't be ridiculous. You can't kill death," Audrey said, as she sauntered back into the dining room holding a decanter in one hand and two snifters in the other, one sloshing brandy.

When I reached out to take that snifter for Kitty, she said, "Oh no, that one's mine." So, I took the decanter and the empty glass from her.

Audrey focused her attention on the brandy and Robert. "Don't you know the Grim Reaper shows up to collect people's souls and then he escorts them from this world."

Robert plopped down in a chair. "That's the first problem. This Grim Reaper is not a male. She's a woman, a woman we know."

The silence in the room was deep and profound. My eyes darted around the room, mentally ticking off the female guests. Everyone was there, except Lisa. But she couldn't have been the black-hooded figure pointing at us. She had been seated at the table. Then who?

With all the flair of a professional actor, Lisa made an entrance from the kitchen holding a tumbler of some sick green liquid.

"Brandy is fine," Lisa said as she knelt down next to Kitty. "But this concoction is guaranteed to restore your body and mental faculties quickly." She touched the glass to Kitty's lips. "Now, drink this, my friend."

Robert got up again and marched around. With a flourish of

his arm, he proclaimed, "I'm telling you. We've seen the death of the Grim Reaper." His bravado barely hid his distress.

I was confused. All the women at the dinner party were present and accounted for. "Robert, who is dead?"

"The figure in the cloak is, was …" His voice cracked as he spoke her name. "Gretchen."

"No," Lorraine breathed.

"It's true," said Robert. "I saw her myself. Blood everywhere. The carving knife sticking out of her chest." Robert turned to Kitty. "I think it was your carving knife."

We all turned toward the now cold roast on the silver platter. The silver meat carving fork in the heavy, ornate Grand Baroque pattern sat next to meat, unused. Its mate, the hefty carving knife was gone. I remembered it was gone after Harold had run outside after the other men. He must have taken it with him.

With a delicate sigh, Kitty fainted away again, leaving Lisa holding the glass.

I was getting concerned about Kitty. How many shocks could a woman in her seventies handle safely? Of course, I'd never admit to her that I thought she was *that old,* but it was a consideration. I glanced out the window, hoping Dr. Greene was heading back to the house, but there was no one to be seen. The doctor, Robert, Carl and Harold had disappeared into the woods.

Lorraine came up behind me and whispered, "Abby, I want you to call the police. Use the landline in the kitchen." I nodded and slipped away as she took charge of the situation. "Let's all sit down. Lisa, get a pillow from the living room for Kitty's head. I don't think she'll be much help to us right now."

It didn't take me long to place the call. I didn't have much to tell the dispatcher except that someone was dead and to send the ambulance and the police. As I slipped back into the dining room, I gave Lorraine a little nod to let her know that I'd completed the call and help was on the way.

As I sat down, I noticed Audrey reaching for a chair, her hand shaking. A little moan escaped her lips. As she sat down, she spoke as if to herself. "This isn't happening. This can't be happening."

"Robert, tell us what you know," commanded Lorraine.

He took a deep drink of water from someone's glass and began. "You all saw it for yourselves, when the hooded figure appeared outside the window. We all scrambled, the men that is, to grab the person pulling this horrible prank." He paused and glanced away. "I saw Harold grab the carving knife. I thought that was an overreaction, but it's his house. We charged out the kitchen door and went to the place where we'd seen the Grim Reaper, but there was no one there. We spread out to catch him before he left the property." He looked to Audrey. "You see, we thought it was a man. Never guessed it was a woman." He took another drink of water. "We ran around like maniacs."

A thin groan came from the floor. Kitty was awake. Lisa helped her into a chair and put the smoothie in front of her. "Were you just like chickens with your heads cut off?" Kitty murmured. It was just like our hostess to find the right cliché and add it to the conversation.

"That's right. We ran around like crazy. Carl, Mr. Soldier Man, called us together and organized the search. Must have been military experience kicking in." Robert caught Lorraine's expression and quickly continued with the story. "He gave us assignments and sent us out to search our sectors. All I could hear were big feet tromping through fallen leaves and branches." A little shiver ran through him. "Then somebody yelled out, Over here! And we all ran toward the voice.

He took a deep breath to steady himself. "And there it was. On the ground. The Grim Reaper. The huge hood had fallen away to reveal a hideous mask, the face of a skeleton. It looked too strange for words."

Robert sank into the back of the chair. "When Harold came up to us all out of breath, he was hot and going on about somebody knocking him down. Twisted his arm or something. Don't think I've ever seen him so angry. When he looked down at the Grim Reaper on the ground, he lost it. Yelled that he'd had enough fun and games. Carl ordered the person to get up." Robert shook his head as if he wanted to erase the next part of his story from his mind. "There was nothing, no response. We stood around making jokes. Guess we were pretty nervous. I know that I had never seen anything like this before. The Reaper didn't move. I don't know who, but someone kicked a foot."

The women in the room gasped a little, everyone but Kitty. All of us must have felt on edge and couldn't tolerate even this little bit of violence. Kitty seemed to be lost in her own world, which wasn't all that unusual.

"Don't get the wrong idea. It was a gentle kick. More like a nudge." He waved his hand in the air as if waving away our concern. "That's not important. Even with a nudge, the person didn't move. Right then, Doctor Greene rushed up and knelt by the body. He laid his fingers on the wrist and then frowned. He moved up to the head and tried to get his fingers underneath the mask.

"He demanded that we get the mask off. That snapped us into action. Harold was the one who pulled the mask free. We all stared while the doctor searched for a pulse."

"Who was this awful person who frightened me?" shrieked Kitty.

Robert turned to her, his expression filled with sadness. "Kitty," he said gently. "It was Gretchen. It was our Gretchen, dressed up as the Grim Reaper."

Kitty's hands flew to her face to cover her mouth wide open in shock.

"Gretchen? How can that be?" said Audrey.

Lisa shook her head in silent surprise.

It was hard to think that someone I knew could do such a thing. I looked to Lorraine, for comfort I guess, but her eyes were cast downward to her hands clasped together on the black tablecloth. I followed her lead and kept my thoughts to myself.

"Robert, you'd better bring that girl here to me right now." Kitty brought her delicate fist down lightly on the dining room table. "I want to know why she would do such a nasty thing."

Robert cleared his throat. "That's not going to happen, Kitty."

Kitty was indignant. "And why not?"

"Doctor Greene couldn't find a pulse. He said our Grim Reaper hadn't fainted." Robert rubbed his face with both hands and shuddered. "He showed us something that I don't think I will ever get out of my brain. He pulled the cloak back from Gretchen's body to reveal a large knife sticking out of her chest. He said, 'I'm afraid our Grim Reaper is dead.'"

"But who was it?" demanded Kitty.

"Oh, for heaven's sake, Kitty. Gretchen. Somebody murdered Gretchen!" Robert's lack of compassion was like a slap across the face.

"Murdered?" Reality had hit Kitty, finally. "Gretchen? Dead?" Kitty's voice was rising to hysterics. "Where's my husband? Where is Harold?"

I realized that the rest of the men were still outside, probably standing guard over the body. Audrey and Lisa went to calm her down while Robert looked at me and Lorraine. We must have seemed, as Kitty would say, like the safe or sane port in the storm.

"I guess the only thing for us to do is to call the police." Robert said.

"Already done," I assured him.

He paused for a moment and frowned. "I just wish…"

"What?" I asked when he fell silent.

"I wish I hadn't heard Harold say, 'I wish I hadn't done that.'"

I jerked back in surprise. Lorraine reached out and gently grabbed my arm.

"What did he mean?" Robert asked us. "Do you think he could have killed her?"

CHAPTER THREE

.

The three-piece roast carving set is used to carve large roasts such as beef, lamb, turkey or other large fowl. The roast carving set includes a roast carving fork, a roast carving knife and a steel or sharpener.

"The Butler's Guide to Fine Silver"
Mr. Hollister, 1898

I'd slipped back into the dining room after making the 911 call using the landline. Lorraine always seemed to have her wits about her in a crisis. Neither one of us remembered the address of the house, but the call coming from the landline would give the police dispatcher accurate information.

"They're on the way. I don't know if the chief is on duty right now, but if he is, he will be with the first responders," I said softly to Lorraine, then hesitated.

"Abby, what's wrong?" she asked quietly.

"What do you think Harold meant?"

"You mean when he said what Robert *thinks* he heard him say?"

"Yes. *I wish I hadn't done that.*" It made me uncomfortable repeating the words of a possible killer.

Lorraine's brow wrinkled. "Do you think he meant he was sorry he killed her?" I nodded. "Oh Abby, we're talking about Harold here. Mild-mannered, almost timid Harold. You'll have to trust me on this one since you don't know them very well. I think if there was a mouse in the room, Harold would be the first one to jump up on a chair. I can't imagine a man like that could plunge a carving knife into someone's body."

I gave her a long look. It hadn't been that long since we'd learned that someone we knew was capable of almost anything. She sighed as if acknowledging that unspoken thought.

"But why?" Lorraine pleaded for an answer. "Why would he do such a horrible thing?"

Now, it was my turn to sigh. "I have no idea. If we could see telltale signs that someone was contemplating murder, there wouldn't be any murders in the world."

"You're right. One never knows. Abby, do you feel comfortable going outside to let the men know that the police are on their way? And take Robert with you. Nobody should be alone right now."

Soon, I was following Robert into the woods. Firm steps crushed the low vegetation. A thought flitted across my mind: what if I was following the killer into the woods? Before I could react, we'd arrived at the place where the men were standing around a mound of black material that lay on the ground. Someone had covered the knife with the cloak again and put a handkerchief over Gretchen's face. I let them know we had called the police, but it really wasn't necessary. We all could hear the sirens in the distance getting louder and louder.

I really wanted to leave this place and go back to the house. "I'd better go back so I can lead the cops out here."

Harold trotted after me. "I'd better come, too. After all, I am the owner of the property."

And maybe the killer, I added silently. I quickened my step.

Just as we got to the house, the police chief's car pulled up the circular driveway. Lorraine came out the front door and walked toward me as Harold scurried inside. The tall man with a broad chest got out of his car. His eyes grew wide and he blinked twice. I think we were the last people he expected to find waiting for him.

Police Chief Luken came over to us. "What are you two doing here?" He touched my arm. "Are you okay? Are you…?"

"No, Chief, we're fine. But Gretchen Mayer, she isn't." I took a moment to catch my breath. I was *not* going to let the tears go now. Gretchen wasn't a close friend, but I knew her. I had loved hearing about how she developed her superhero adventures and the intricacies of translating them into comic book form. I liked her. She seemed like a good person. She didn't deserve to die, not like this, lying in the middle of the woods with a carving knife sticking out of her body. I wasn't going to let my emotions rule me now. Later, maybe, but not now. "Chief, I'm afraid you've got a murder on your hands."

"I got that impression from the 911 call. After the dispatcher notified my officers on duty, she routed the info to me. I've already alerted Homicide Detective Ingram and he's on his way."

"You've got a wide array of suspects," I said with a nervous smile that twitched.

"Oh good, just what I need." His mahogany skin glinted in the waning light of the evening. He took off his policeman's cap, ran his hand over his short-cropped black hair and settled the cap back in place. "Guess I'd better get started." He headed toward the front door.

I called out. "But the good news is…" The Chief paused. "The obvious suspects are all inside the house or in the woods with the body. The case is all tied up with a bow. You just have to identify the killer."

He turned to me and a broad smile spread over his face, his chocolate eyes twinkling. "Well then, maybe this'll be a little easier than I thought."

More sirens were coming our way and the official vehicles turned up the driveway: two police cruisers and an ambulance. I hadn't meant to become the emergency response traffic cop, but I was able to direct one officer inside to join the Chief then I found

Robert to lead the other officer and paramedics to the woods where the body lay. Everybody had a job to do, but me. I made my way back inside where Lorraine and several other guests were sitting at the dining table playing with the flatware or staring into space, trying to process what was happening. Audrey nervously paced around the room, stopping at the window to catch sight of any action outside.

It wasn't long before the men from the woods came in and the Chief asked everyone to sit down.

"Ladies and gentlemen, this is a very sad situation, one that makes you uncomfortable and thinking of only going home. However, we have a problem. I have to start an investigation into the manner of this young woman's death and I need your help. So, I'm afraid I'm going to have to ask you all to make yourselves comfortable for a little while. My officers will gather your contact information and then we need to await the arrival of the investigating detective."

The room erupted in a cacophony of questions and demands, but the Chief didn't lose a beat. His deep resonant voice took command. "Yes, I know, but we have to follow protocol out of respect for the woman who just lost her life."

Kitty's hesitant voice piped up from the end of the table. "Chief, was it… Was it murder?"

"Yes, Mrs. Fitzgerald, I feel fairly certain that it is. That's why we need to get statements from you all while events are still fresh in your minds."

"When is this detective going to show up?" barked Carl.

"I notified Homicide and they let me know that Detective Ingram is on his way. In the meantime, if everyone would have a seat, we can collect your contact information."

"Chief?" It was Kitty again moving back into her role of hostess. "Do you think we could at least take the food off the table?" she said as she waved a fly away.

The chief exchanged looks with an officer. "I think we should wait until the detective arrives. He shouldn't be much longer."

Dr. Greene stumbled into the room, the last of the stragglers from the woods and looked a little surprised to see everyone gathered there. "Oh, excuse me. I—"

An officer approached him as the Chief said, "Are you alright?"

"Y-yes. Yes, I'm fine."

"You're the doctor who checked the body?"

"Yes. I should be used to seeing dead bodies, but it's different when it's someone you know." He raised his hands a little. There were traces of blood on his fingers. "I just want to wash up."

The Chief nodded and the doctor left the room.

People sat quietly, not wanting to talk. We listened to the mumblings of the officers taking down the contact information from the guests. The tense atmosphere in the room snapped when an unmarked car drew up to the front door, making the gravel driveway growl.

Kitty jumped up. "Now, who in the world could that be?"

The Chief stopped her. "That's all right. I'll take care of it. If you would please sit down again." He gestured to the hostess chair at the end of the table. Reluctantly, Kitty sat down.

The Chief went to the door and I could hear him talking with Detective Ingram. I knew I'd never forget the voice of the man who once thought I'd committed murder. They spoke in low tones, too low to understand what they were saying. It wasn't long before they entered the dining room.

The Chief began. "Ladies and gentlemen, this is Homicide Detective Ingram. He will be leading the investigation." The detective, just under six feet tall with thin brown hair sprinkled with gray, stepped up to the head of the table. He looked tired, but I knew it wasn't because of the late evening hour. This man had seen too much over his career and those situations had taken a toll. "Good evening, everyone. As the Chief said, my name is Ingram. I'm sorry that we have to meet under these circumstances. I ask your indulgence while I check out the crime scene and then I will be back to talk with all of you." Robert started to object, but Ingram shut him down. "I believe I said I will be back as soon as I can. Chief, with me." Quickly, he turned to leave, but not quickly enough.

Kitty stood. "Detective, may I have a word with you please?"

"Ma'am, I—"

"It will only take a moment." She walked out to the hall, assured that he would follow. After a moment's hesitation, he did. It didn't take long for them to return from their consultation and Kitty addressed her guests. "Dear friends, the detective has given us permission to continue our dinner party. Shall we move to the patio where we will have coffee and a little dessert to keep our energy up? If you'll follow me…" She led the way through a pair of French doors and down to the pool area.

I was surprised that Kitty recovered so well and so quickly, but she had the job of taking care of her guests and she was going to do it. A few of the guests glanced at the detective for confirmation. He gave a slight nod and left with the Chief. Before Lorraine and I were out of our chairs, the Chief was back wiggling his index finger for us to follow him. Outside, the four of us stood in a small circle.

"Good evening, Mrs. Andrews," Ingram said to Lorraine. "And good evening to you, Abby."

"Detective, I thought we decided that you could call me Lorraine. After all we've been through, it seems appropriate." She was referring, of course, to the murder of her dear friend Evelyn just months before the dinner party and the part we both played in identifying her killer.

He nodded slowly. "But this is a little different situation. I'm afraid your presence here puts you on the list of suspects."

I was expecting that, but seeing Lorraine's hand touch her chest with a little gasp, it was obvious that she hadn't seen that coming. I mentally kicked myself for getting her involved in this pleasant dinner with her friends, but it was too late to change anything. We had to deal with things as they were.

"However, I would like to ask you both a question." We stood silently waiting. "Did either one of you have anything to do with the murder of this young woman?"

"No!" We said in unison.

The detective smiled. "That's what I thought. I need to look at the crime scene and then I'd like to interview both of you first."

We agreed and, as he walked away, I had to stifle a giggle. If it was that easy for me, us, to avoid suspicion in a murder case… Hmm-m-m, I'd have to remember that.

CHAPTER FOUR

The roast carving knife has a long, narrow blade that tapers to a sharp point so it easily cuts through dense meat and around bone. The metal feet at the handle keeps the blade off the tablecloth when the knife is not in use.

"The Butler's Guide to Fine Silver"
Mr. Hollister, 1898

The police officers directed us down to the massive blue flagstone patio surrounding the swimming pool. People seemed happier, more relaxed, to have someplace to go, something to do. It was too cool for swimming of course, but it was nice to look at the blue water and statuary decorating the area. A Grecian woman of stone held an urn of rushing water and the statue of a little boy added *water* to the hot tub. It was something to do. It was better than being cooped up inside. Fortunately, it was still warm enough to sit outside comfortably and the hot coffee and little desserts helped as well.

Lorraine and I wandered over to a quiet spot where several

white Adirondack chairs sat around a small table near a stand of majestic pine trees. We wanted to forget what was happening around us and watch the sunset, an event that never bored my friend. The briefing we gave Detective Ingram when he returned from the crime scene exhausted Lorraine. To be honest, it took a toll on me, too. Once the adrenaline rush triggered by sudden death and fear wore off, I was truly ready to lie down.

I thought back to the discussion we'd had with the Chief and Detective Ingram. It was short, but fascinating. We told them we didn't know much of anything that would be helpful. Ingram rejected that idea and pushed forward. He said that people often knew more than they thought. One of the police officers had made a list of the potential suspects for him and he had us go through it.

The list included the cook and her kitchen helper. They each provided an alibi for the other so Ingram struck their names off the list. We went over the rest of the names and struck some from the list as well, because those people never left the dining room and therefore had no opportunity to stab poor Gretchen.

At first, all the women were taken off the list, but, on second thought, Ingram asked us to go through each name one by one. Kitty, Lorraine and I never left the dining room so, we supplied alibis for each other. But two other names stayed on the list. After Kitty fainted, Audrey left the room to get the decanter of brandy and two snifters. Thinking back, it seemed to me that she'd been gone for quite a while. Was it long enough to sprint outside, find Gretchen and stab her? It seemed a little extreme so I didn't say anything since he included her as a suspect. Then there was Lisa, the chef. She slipped into the kitchen and made a restorative smoothie for Kitty. It took time to make it, especially when she wasn't in her own kitchen and had to scare up the ingredients. Again, was it long enough to go outside and kill Gretchen? But the cook and her helper must have been in the kitchen, too, so Ingram could confirm Lisa's whereabouts.

There was the list of men, all of them considered suspects. When the Grim Reaper appeared, they had all jumped up and run to grab the person playing a terrible practical joke. They told the detective that when they reached the area where the figure first appeared, they found nothing. Carl, the retired military man, organized a search. It was probably in those next few minutes that somebody had come upon Gretchen and stabbed her. The killer could easily melt back into the shadows of the woods and respond when somebody else found her.

I wondered why no one heard her scream, but the Chief came up with some logical suggestions.

"The killer could have put his hand over her mouth. Also, someone is more likely to scream when seeing another person being stabbed. Think of it this way, to scream you need to take a deep breath and if you have a knife in your chest, that's really gonna hurt."

He was right. I felt a little silly.

"I think the key will be figuring out the motive," Ingram said. "Why would someone want to kill Gretchen Mayer?"

"But Detective," Lorraine interjected. "I think you need to find out why Gretchen would appear dressed as the Grim Reaper outside the dining room window, pointing to someone at the table."

Ingram nodded. "That's a very important point, Lorraine. Any ideas?"

Slowly, she had shaken her head.

Now, Lorraine and I sat quietly, alone with our thoughts. I hoped the detective would let us go home soon. After all the initial excitement, waiting around was more than boring, but the niggling thought that there was probably a killer among us kept me on edge.

"Mind if I join you?" Dr. Greene said, standing tall over us, blocking the setting sun. He was balancing a coffee cup and saucer and a slice of chocolate chiffon pie on a small dessert plate.

I had to crane my head back to see his face. He must have been well over six feet tall. There was something about him, but I couldn't put my finger on it. Maybe he seemed a little too casual and comfortable for the circumstances with his jacket off and his sleeves rolled up. Or maybe I was being overly critical, protective of Lorraine. If she wanted him to join us, who was I to stand in her way?

"Of course, you can join us, Doctor Greene. Let me help you." I took his coffee and set it on the small table. It didn't hurt to have a good-looking man close to Lorraine's age keeping us company. I knew she wouldn't appreciate my little matchmaking ploy, so I made no move to leave the two of them alone, at least not yet. She didn't have to marry him for heaven's sake, but a little distraction wouldn't be so bad.

I put the brakes on those thoughts. I'd been wrong about this dinner party being a nice distraction from the sadness of Evie's murder. I might be wrong about this man, too.

Lorraine settled back. "You look much more relaxed now, Doctor Greene."

"Please call me James. And yes, I took off my jacket and rolled up my sleeves when I went to wash up after…" He paused for a moment. "After I made that sad determination in the woods. I'm afraid it was a rather messy situation and I didn't want to bring that back to the party. It's good to feel the breeze on my arms." He turned to Lorraine and started talking about the weather, the changes from the extreme summer temperatures to the more pleasant autumn days and the predictions for the upcoming winter.

I was grateful that he shifted the topic of conversation away from the murder. He seemed to only have eyes for Lorraine, so I gave him the once-over that might have seemed rude in another situation, but I was curious about this man who had caught the eye of my friend.

His blonde hair, cut longish to look windblown, was streaked by the sun, but I wasn't sure if that wasn't done in a salon, because what doctor has a lot of time to spend outside? The one thing that impressed me was the way he carried himself. Not wooden like the retired military man, Carl. The only way I could describe it was that the doctor respected himself and was comfortable with who he was. Yes, that summed him up. He was comfortable with himself,

I tuned back into their conversation. "…and I love to come down and borrow Harold's little sailboat. I lose myself out there with only the wind and water."

So, he did get his sun-streaked hair honestly. I scolded myself. Maybe I was being suspicious because I wanted to protect my friend. I resolved to guard my tongue. Lorraine could certainly make her own decisions about new friends, especially men.

The doctor smiled. "I found it interesting to watch the little tussle you two had at the table. It was very entertaining." Lorraine and I exchanged looks. "Don't worry, your secret is safe with me and, for what it's worth, I think you did the right thing."

I started to ask him what he was talking about, but he held up his hand.

"I'm talking about whether you should have said anything about the placement of the cocktail fork in the place settings."

He caught Lorraine so flatfooted that she almost spewed the sip of coffee she'd just taken from the delicate china cup. I was impressed with how quickly she recovered without missing a ladylike beat.

"You both were polite and courteous, something in short supply these days," he said. "There's no question that she made a mistake putting the cocktail fork on the left side of the plate. It was obvious."

Lorraine and I exchanged a look of thinly veiled surprise.

"And in doing so," he continued, "she also broke the rule of no more than three forks on the left."

I could feel my jaw starting to drop. Not many people today knew the proper placement of a cocktail fork. Even fewer knew of the Only Three Forks rule.

He gave us a bright smile. "My mother."

Lorraine nodded in silent understanding.

"She loved using china, crystal and most of all, sterling silver in the dining room." He looked down into his coffee cup, remembering. "She thought it was part of a sophisticated gentleman's education to know such things."

Lorraine smiled back. "I think I'd like your mother very much."

"You two have a lot in common, but I didn't come over here to talk about my mother. I'm afraid we got interrupted just as you were about to tell a scary story, Lorraine. I'm interested because you said the story still sent a shiver through you, and I was wondering why."

Lorraine glanced away, almost embarrassed, then looked up at him again. "I first heard the story when I was a little girl about eight years old. My friend Evie was ten. I know that children that age are impressionable, but we both refused to walk by a cemetery for years."

"What did you do? There are two cemeteries right in the middle of the shopping district of St. Michaels," the doctor asked, genuinely interested.

"We crossed the street, of course," Lorraine said with a nervous little laugh.

He looked around at the others waiting to be called for an interview as the police began their investigation. "It seems we have nothing to do, but wait. Would you tell your story now?"

"Well, I guess. If you really want to hear it?" Lorraine said, almost embarrassed.

He nodded. "Yes, yes, I would. Not because I like being scared, but it's sort of a hobby of mine to search out a plausible explanation to mysteries." He settled back in an Adirondack chair. "You have a captive audience so, please begin."

I noticed her eyes glazing over as she went to another place, another time.

My best friend Evie and I scooted to either side of the old woman known as the storyteller. She sat on the edge of the dock and we all dangled our feet over the water of the St. Michaels Harbor. She smelled of seafood and sweat. We didn't care. We only wanted to hear every word of the story she was telling us.

"...and she died. This woman, Miss Hanna, she was the preacher's wife, real young and strong. But that didn't save her. No sir-ee. Nothing could save her." The old woman leaned in close to me, her crooked nose almost touching my nose. "She died... or did she?"

It was an August afternoon, sweaty hot. But I shivered as if someone had thrown an icy blanket over me. This old woman and her stories always had that effect on me.

"Wh-what happened to her?" I asked, my voice cracking.

"Like I said, she died. They put her in a plain pine box and took her to the church. Her husband said the funeral service over her, him being the pastor and all. Then they made up this procession and followed the coffin out to the graveyard."

I gasped. This was going to be the really scary part. I wanted to cover my ears, but I didn't. The woman swung her weathered face around and peered deep into my eyes. So deep that it felt like a spike going straight into my soul. I squeezed my eyes shut.

"What's the matter, girlie?" the woman growled. "'fraid already? Maybe you oughta run right home to Momma 'cause ya ain't gonna like the rest of the story."

"No, Rainey," Evie called out. "Please don't go!"

My friend wanted, needed me to stay. I opened my eyes slowly then I threw back my shoulders. I looked directly at the old woman and said in a voice that I hoped sounded braver than I felt, "Please continue. We'd like to hear the rest of the story."

The old woman was taken aback by the formal tone my momma had taught me to use with grownups, but resettled herself on the weathered wood of the dock as if nothing had happened. "Well now, where was I?"

Evie responded, a little too eagerly for my taste. "They were going to the graveyard."

"That's right. Now, the people filed out of the church to follow the coffin to an open pit dug in the middle of all the tombstones."

She cackled. "And if you'd 'ave been there and looked over the edge into the hole, you might 'ave seen a clump of dirt come loose from the wall of the grave and fall all the way to the bottom. There would 'ave been a little splash, 'cause it had rained the night before."

Evie's high-pitched squeal sent ripples of dread down my back. She finally gasped out the words, "You mean they were going to put her coffin in a puddle of water?"

The idea made me shiver.

"Why, sure. The preacher's wife, Miss Hanna, didn't care, 'cause she was deaaad!" The woman dragged out that last word so it sounded creepy.

I knew she was trying to scare us. It wasn't nice. Even knowing this, I was still scared. I had to be brave for my friend.

The old woman coughed and took some water from a chipped cup. "The men, they gathered around the open grave. Not the preacher, mind you. He stood at the head of the grave and recited the prayers for his dearly departed wife's soul, 'cause there was no one else to lead the service. And when he was done, the men let out the ropes that lowered the coffin into the hole."

Evie jumped up, ran around and plopped down next to me, grabbed my hand and held on tight. I didn't know which one of us was more scared, but it didn't matter. We were quaking together.

"Do you know what happened then?" our storyteller asked. We shook our heads so hard, our hair whipped in our faces.

"Well, I'll tell you. A couple of the men grabbed shovels and stood by the mound of dirt they'd dug out of the hole. And they waited."

"Waited for what?" I asked, not sure I wanted to hear the answer.

"For the people to leave, of course. Nobody wants to see dirt tossed down onto the top of a casket. And they don't want to hear it neither, the thud—thud—thuds."

I could feel the shiver run through Evie's body right down her arm from her hand to mine. Was Evie remembering her momma's funeral when she was a little girl? I squeezed it to let her know I was still with her.

"Then what happened? Where did all the people go?" Evie asked. The girl was full of questions.

"Why, the people went on over to the preacher's house for a wake. Know what that is?" We shook our heads. "It's when people get together to eat and drink and remember the person who done passed on. Sometimes, they have a wake before the funeral. They bring the casket right into the house and take the top off so everybody can see the body. Then they make a whole lot of noise. They tell stories, they laugh, they sing songs at the top of their lungs."

I cringed. "Why?"

"'cause it's a *wake!* They try to wake the dearly departed, in case they ain't really dead."

"Oh, no," I breathed.

"But in the case of Miss Hanna, they waited until after the funeral to have the wake so the body was in the ground, not in the house." The old woman got quiet, quiet like the dead, and looked down at the water. She mumbled something, but I caught every word. "Guess they should have done it the other way 'round."

"Why?" We asked in unison.

The old woman narrowed her eyes and looked at me from under her wild eyebrows. "'cause of what happened."

Evie and I leaned closer to each other.

"While the congregation was doing the funeral, out in the woods, two men, mangy characters they were, lurkin' in the shadows, watching." She drew close to Evie and looked deep into her eyes. Then turned to me. I could have sworn she saw clear to the back of my skull.

"They watched everything and waited until they all walked away to the preacher's house."

"Who were they, the men?" asked Evie in a voice that suggested she wasn't sure she wanted to know the answer.

"Oh, they were a bad sort. They got into so much trouble down Shore, they were makin' for Baltimore to get work. Maybe even to sign on one of those big ships that go to exotic places.

They had big plans, but could never make 'em happen. They were a bad luck sort like that."

"Why were they hanging around the cemetery?" I asked. "Sounds like they were looking for trouble."

"Trouble?" She cocked her head then shook it. "No, they were looking for treasure."

"Treasure?" said Evie. "In a cemetery?"

The old woman looked at her up and down, from head to toe. "You're a smart one, ain't ya? Wanna know everything. All rightie then. You see, back then, people liked to be buried with something special to 'em."

I piped up. "Like what?"

"Oh, maybe a nice dress or a Sunday go-to-church suit. Lots of times, it was somethin' valuable like a watch or broach."

"Why?"

She shrugged her shoulders. "Heck if I know. Seems a waste to me. Ya don't need nothin' when ya leave this world. The men didn't know Miss Hanna, but they wanted to find out. If there was somethin' in that grave, they figured that she didn't need it 'cause she was dead."

I wished the woman would stop saying that. When she did, I felt cold tingles like someone was watching us, but when I looked around, no one was there.

"What did they do?" Evie wanted to know.

"They waited real quiet like, until everybody left. Then they moved from one shadow to the next, silent as a ghost. Only the dry leaves gave away their footsteps. Then they dashed to the fresh grave, took one more look around to be sure they were alone then grabbed the two shovels left there."

"Then what did they do?"

"They started digging."

"NO!" Evie and I screamed.

"Oh yes, they did. They used those shovels and dug and dug… the dirt flying up in the air and out of the grave. They dug and dug until they hit wood."

Evie and I huddled together, holding each other's hands, afraid of what was coming next.

"They took the pointy end of those shovels and jammed 'em into the top of the coffin. The wood broke apart and they could see the poor woman's body. Sunlight that was never to touch her skin again fell on her face, white as flour. Her hands were folded over her chest and that's where they found the treasure."

"What was it?" we sang out in unison.

"There on the third finger of her right hand was a silver ring. They said her mother gave it to her when she was on her death bed. Hanna wore it all the time, never took it off and when she was real sick, she told her husband she wanted to be buried with it. So, he honored her wishes."

"Did those awful men take the ring?"

She shifted her body and groaned a little. "Well, they tried. But Hanna's hand was frozen with death and they couldn't get it off."

"They left it alone, right?" I said, hoping it was true.

The woman sat back and looked at me in disbelief. "Are you crazy? These men were after the treasure. They weren't going to let a little thing like a stiff finger keep them from getting what they wanted."

Evie moved her head closer to the woman. "What did they do?"

"The big man took out his knife and set about to cut off her finger."

We screamed and threw our arms around each other in horror.

The woman kept on. "But a finger, a dead finger at that, ain't the easiest thing to cut off. He had to dig around with his knife and blood went everywhere. When he hit bone, he had to start sawing away."

I took a deep breath, relieved that this horrid story was over. "So, they got the ring,"

But the woman was shaking her head slowly. "Nope, that ain't what happened." When she was sure she had our attention again, she said, "They never got the ring, because Miss Hanna sat straight up in her coffin, eyes wide."

We jumped up in shock. "How is that possible?"

The woman shrugged. "Guess Miss Hanna wasn't ready to give up her momma's ring. She came back to life to make sure no one took it from her."

"What did the men do?"

She yawned as if bored with the story now. "I imagine they screamed their heads off, jumped out of the grave and ran away like the silly fools they were."

Evie took a deep breath. "A-a-and what happened to Miss Hanna?"

"Well, she wasn't dead no more, was she? She didn't belong in the cemetery no more. So, she got herself out of that grave and walked over to the house where she and the preacher lived. She went up to the door and knocked." The old woman leaned down and rapped on the wood dock once, twice, three times. They sent a tremor through us.

Evie gulped. "Then what happened?"

For the first time, she smiled, showing a gap in her front teeth. "Why she walked right into her house and took up living her life like before she died. They say she had more children, but the scars on her finger never went away. But that's not the end of the story."

"No, it must be." I couldn't take anymore.

"They say if you go to the old White Marsh Church when the moon is right, you can see Miss Hanna walking home from the cemetery, blood still dripping from her finger."

Lorraine's eyes focused on us again. She was back from that time so long ago. "Right then, Evie's daddy came along and threw a fit that the old woman was scaring us with her crazy stories. She claimed they weren't crazy. He told us to pay no mind to her stories. But that was easier said than done." She took a sip of her cold coffee.

"And the story of Hanna and her ring kept us both awake for many nights. During the day, whenever we were walking on

Talbot Street in the middle of St. Michaels and we came to the cemetery around Christ Church, we'd cross the street. What if another Hanna, dead and buried, came back to life? It's a thought that still haunts me a little to this day."

Doctor Greene looked at Lorraine and smiled, a smile filled with compassion and comfort. "I believe there might be a simple explanation for what happened in your story. Would you like to hear it?"

Lorraine sat forward. "Yes, yes I would."

"Then why don't I get us some fresh coffee and I'll tell you what I think really happened." He looked over to me as if he suddenly remembered I was sitting there. "Abby, I'm sorry I only have two hands."

"That's okay, I'll go with you and get my own."

It didn't take long for us to refill our cups and settle back in the chairs. I could understand why Lorraine and Evie had been terrified as children. It would be interesting to hear the doctor's rational explanation.

"Do you realize your story is probably true?" asked the doctor.

Lorraine frowned a little in surprise. "True? Because it is told so often?"

"No, because it was not that unusual for people to be buried alive in that period of our history."

"What?!" I burst out.

"Granted, it wasn't that common, but it did happen."

"How can that be?" I wanted to know.

"It was difficult for people to tell the difference between death and coma in the 1700 and 1800's. The conditions look remarkably similar."

I was a little surprised when Lorraine encouraged him to go on. I thought she'd had her fill of death and funerals, but I was wrong.

"If you think about it, a person in a coma acts ... or should I say doesn't react ...like a living human being," he explained. "The person doesn't respond to speech or loud noise. There's no reaction to outside stimulus like a pinch or needle pricks. If you look into the eyes, there's no dilation of the pupil. Respiration may be so shallow that it couldn't be discerned by their crude methods of finding respiration or heartbeat."

"Is that why the Irish tradition includes a wake?" I asked.

"Very astute. Some say it is an old wives' tale, but I'm not sure. The Irish used to love drinking their stout from pewter tankards, which often resulted in lead poisoning that could cause a catatonic state or coma. It looked like the person died. They held a wake in honor of the deceased…" The doctor made air quotation marks. "… all the while watching for signs of a reawakening. If the cause of the coma is exposure to lead, the person may recover after a few hours or even a couple days."

"Hence the name *wake*. I get it now," I said.

He turned to Lorraine. "So, dear lady, the story that frightened you so badly as a child might have been true. You said the woman had suffered from an illness. It might have been a viral infection with high fever, for example. Her body went into a coma to heal and the people in the rural community assumed she had died. She was truly fortunate that graverobbers moved in so quickly."

Lorraine shifted her gaze to the setting sun, trying to take in the information. "Is that possible?" A shiver ran through her. "It's almost scarier to think that she could have remained in that coffin until she died."

He nodded sadly. "Some people did. There are stories of expensive caskets, during removal to make way for construction projects, being opened to reveal the elegant lining of the box being torn to shreds and the fingernails of the corpse being broken and bloody." He drew a deep breath. "But let's not think of that. Just know that sometimes, there is truth behind the scary stories."

He rose and said to Lorraine, "Shall we take a little walk around the house, away from the woods?" He added specifically. "Perhaps we could get some more coffee? I'm not sure why I feel so tired. I guess the events of this day plus my speech at the Ocean City convention center took more out of me than I thought."

I watched, with a barely hidden smile, as Lorraine and Dr. Greene walked away together.

CHAPTER FIVE

The butler has the responsibility to help protect the silver of the House and to protect the House from fakes and forgeries of silver pieces. There are simple techniques to use to detect a fraudulent piece. For example, each hallmark must be applied individually by the maker. If the marks line up perfectly, one has reason to be suspicious.

"The Butler's Guide to Fine Silver"
Mr. Hollister, 1898

"Oh, Abby, I need you." Kitty was all aflutter. "The Chief wants to question me, you know, one-on-one and I simply can't do it alone."

I rose from the Adirondack chair with difficulty. It was not designed for a person to get out of gracefully. I finally got to my feet and took Kitty's hand. "You have nothing to worry about. Lorraine and I were with you the whole time. The Chief can't suspect you of murder. We are your alibi."

"I know, I know. It's just that I don't want to get anyone in trouble."

"Kitty," I added with a stern tone. "Somebody got into trouble when he or she…" I stopped. I didn't want to say *Sunk your carving knife into Gretchen's body.* That would have sent Kitty into another fit of hysterics. So, I tempered what I had to say. "… got into trouble by doing this awful thing."

She patted my arm. "Of course, you're right. It's just that Harold can't be with me." Her voice went right up the scale. "They think he's a suspect, Abby."

"Kitty, take a deep breath. You will get through this."

"Yes, I know. That's why I asked the Chief if you and Lorraine could sit with me during his interrogation."

Oh dear. I hated the idea of interrupting Lorraine's time with Dr. Greene, but she could manage Kitty much better than I could. We went to gather up Lorraine and met with the Chief in the cozy breakfast nook off the kitchen.

He began. "First, have you seen any strangers hanging around the property recently? Anyone suspicious looking?"

Kitty's hand holding a lace trimmed handkerchief flew to her mouth. "No, was there someone?" She grabbed Lorraine's arm. "Were we sitting ducks?"

Quickly, the Chief headed off the drama. "No, I don't know of anyone. I was wondering if you'd seen anything out of the ordinary?"

Kitty shook her head, fear tamped down for the moment. "As you may remember, I fainted." She added softly to herself, "Very embarrassing for a hostess to do." She took a deep breath and looked at the Chief. "If you want to know what was happening, you should ask Audrey. That girl never misses a trick."

The Chief nodded. "Okay, but right now, tell me about the two cooks in the kitchen." He checked his notebook. "Carolanne and Rose."

Kitty was horrified. "There is no way they would hurt a fly, let alone kill someone. They are the sweetest…" Recovering her wits, she straightened up in her chair. "If nothing else, Chief, they were too busy in the kitchen with the dessert, Chocolate Soufflé. A soufflé must be prepared carefully, put in the oven at just the right time and served immediately when it is done. There's no way they could go outside and kill someone."

She looked away and sighed. "I assumed it was a result of Gretchen's murder. Silly me."

The Chief closed his eyes and rubbed his forehead. "You're losing me."

"Oh, I'm sorry. I thought you knew. With all the commotion, the soufflé fell." Kitty jumped up from her chair. "But if you want something, I can get you—"

Lorraine gently grabbed her hand and guided her back into her seat. "You can give him something to eat later."

"Chief, those ladies in the kitchen couldn't have done it," I declared. "The murder weapon was the silver carving knife, right?" The Chief nodded. "It was on the table by the standing rib roast. Neither woman came into the dining room after delivering the main course. The cooks are in the clear."

"I have to check out all possibilities. The only person who admits to having the knife outside is Harold and—"

"Outside?" Kitty interrupted. "That's not possible. Harold didn't leave the dining room."

The Chief countered, "Yes, I'm afraid he did."

"He couldn't have," she shot back. "He would never have left my side. He would never have left me prostrate on the floor after seeing that awful thing outside."

The Chief glanced at me for support. "I'm afraid more than one person told me that he went outside and took the knife with him."

"Then you were told wrong! My husband would never have left me in that condition."

The Chief looked to Lorraine for help.

She took the older, distraught woman's hand. "Now, Kitty, we've told you how chaotic things were. People didn't know what to do and—"

"Whoever said Harold left me, lied," Kitty insisted.

Lorraine cleared her throat gently. "Kitty," she began gently. "Harold told the Chief he went outside."

The woman reeled with the news. The Chief came forward, afraid she would faint.

Somehow, she got herself under control again. "Well, if it did happen that way, he must have known I was alright." Her eyes welled up with tears. "But he didn't have the knife. He couldn't have killed her."

The Chief leaned forwarded to head off the coming torrent, but it was Lorraine's stern words that did the trick.

"Kitty! Just because he admits to taking the knife outside doesn't mean he did anything with it."

"That's right," the Chief agreed. "He did say that someone knocked him down and he dropped the knife. When he got up, he ran off without it."

"Did he see who knocked him down? Maybe that person took the knife…" I glanced at Kitty. "… and used it."

"Unfortunately, no. He has no idea who ran into him. Whoever it was came up from behind and pushed him to the ground."

Kitty smashed her fist into her lap, quite over the tears. "Oh, that's just like Harold. Can't see the nose on his face."

We all did a double-take. It's almost impossible to see one's own nose, but Kitty was the queen of clichés and could do a good job of mangling them, too.

"Alright," the Chief said soothingly. "Miss Kitty, you know these people."

"Yes, yes, I do. They've all been to our home many times."

"Good, so who do you think had a reason to kill Gretchen?"

I could see horror and excitement doing battle across her face. Imagining that she would know a real murderer was the kind of thing Kitty could milk at many upcoming social events. The invitations would be endless.

She cleared her throat, getting down to business as she would say. "Chief, I certainly don't believe that any of my guests, my friends, would hurt Gretchen … or kill her." She paused. Just as the Chief opened his mouth to speak, she hurried on, not ready to give up the spotlight. "And I certainly don't want to cast suspicion on someone who doesn't deserve it. It would be horrible to accuse an innocent person of a crime." She paused again.

The Chief raised his eyebrows. "But…"

"But there may be one or two things you should know, not that they will be helpful in your inquiries."

"Let me be the judge of that. Go on."

"Well, if the rumors are to be believed, Robert is capable of unsavory actions." She paused yet again, but this time, the Chief waited silently. "It was in all the papers." She looked at Lorraine then at me for confirmation, but received none. "It was reported in the financial papers at least. Harold reads them and pointed out the articles to me. I'm sure you've heard of Chamberlain Industries. It was started by Robert's father and uncle and has done *very* well, if you know what I mean. It's still a privately held company so they can do just about anything they want. It appears that his father has done things that Robert doesn't agree with."

"Like what?" the Chief asked as he scribbled notes.

"Pushing the uncle out with less than a fair buyout… and firing older workers in favor of younger ones who cost less." The Chief's pen stopped.

Kitty leaned forward and patted the Chief's hand. "Now, you write down what I'm about to tell you." Not one to be manipulated, the Chief waited. "Well, as we all know, Robert complained to his father who responded by firing his own son and taking him out of the line of succession." She lowered her voice. "You see, Robert was supposed to take over the company when his father retires next year. When Robert started to argue with him, his sister was promoted in his place." Kitty sat back and pronounced judgment. "His father is such a mean-spirited man." A smile crossed her lips. "But Robert is fair and innovative. He went off and started his own venture."

"To compete with his own family's company? Was that necessary?" I exclaimed.

"I don't understand all these things, but yes, I think so."

"This seems straightforward, Miss Kitty," the Chief stated.

She leaned forward again. "Yes, but there is a rumor that Robert took some critical thingie with him. An allegory, no." Her face creased in confusion.

"An algorithm?" I suggested.

"Yes! That's it… what she said. It's supposed to be key to the family's operation, something he'd just developed. And…" She grinned a malevolent grin. "And his sister doesn't know." She sat back in her chair and folded her arms, pleased with herself.

The Chief stopped writing and just looked at Kitty. A frown creased his forehead. "Are you suggesting that his sister came down here and murdered Gretchen?"

Kitty threw up her hands in exasperation and leaned forward again to explain. "No, Chief. I doubt very much she would do that, but…" She paused for effect. "Robert and Gretchen dated for a while. You know that things are shared pillow to pillow that would never be mentioned in the kitchen, living room or anywhere else."

"Do you think Gretchen knew about this …" He didn't know quite what to call it.

Kitty leaned back in her chair again. "Who do you think told me?"

"Do you think Robert was afraid that Gretchen would tell his sister and get him into deep trouble?"

"I don't know, but the one thing I know for sure is that Gretchen was drowning in college loan debt. In fact, Harold and I helped her out on more than one occasion when she couldn't make the whole payment. She couldn't seem to get her head above water."

"Would you say she was desperate for money?"

"Chief, you know how worrying it can be when one can't pay the bills? She kept saying, *If I can only hang on until I develop my superhero.* She was a comic book cartoonist, you know."

"No, I didn't know. But aren't those dreams about hitting it big with your own superhero just dreams?"

"I imagine so, but she made her presentation to the publisher and they wanted her to do a whole workup, I don't know what they call it in the comic book world. She explained it to me that it would be like a pilot in television. She was so excited. She just needed enough money to take care of her bills for a couple of months so she could focus on Radiance, that's the name of her superheroine. She asked us for help, but she wanted more than Harold and I could handle right now, especially after all the other money we'd given her. We were so sorry, but she said not to worry. She had other ways to get the money."

"Maybe Robert was only one of her targets," the Chief mused.

"Targets, Chief?"

"Targets for blackmail."

Kitty's hand shot to her chest in surprise. "Blackmail? Oh, Chief, what a distasteful idea."

"But was she capable of it, Miss Kitty?" He waited for an answer. "You knew her well. You were her confidant."

"Chief, you have to understand—" Kitty's tense voice, taut as a piano wire, squeezed of all her natural Southern hospitality.

The Chief repeated. "Was she capable of blackmail?"

Reluctantly, Kitty nodded her head slowly.

CHAPTER SIX

A piece of jewelry made of sterling silver needs special attention. When it is handled by bare fingers, body oils are transferred to the surface that can cause tarnish, even damage to the piece.

"The Butler's Guide to Fine Silver"
Mr. Hollister, 1898

Moments after Kitty made that unsettling admission, she was escorted out by an officer. Lorraine and I sat without making a sound. We had a front row seat on the investigation and it certainly was more interesting than sitting outside waiting for something to happen. I hoped we wouldn't be asked to leave. Presently, an officer brought Audrey into the room to meet with the Chief. He gestured to the chair for her to sit down, but she refused.

"Why am I here? I didn't do anything," Audrey insisted.

Her reaction raised the Chief's eyebrows in surprise at the strength of her denial. "I never said you did. I just want to ask you a couple of questions."

"I don't know anything." She moved toward the door to leave.

"That's not what your friend said."

She whirled around. "Who?"

"Kitty." The Chief wasn't doing much to calm Audrey or allay her fears. It was a tactic I hadn't seen him use before.

She came closer to the chair in front of the Chief. "What did she say?" she demanded, then a little nervous laugh escaped her lips. "What would she know? She was passed out on the floor." She turned and headed back toward the door.

"She said, 'You should ask Audrey what happened. That girl doesn't miss a thing.' I think I got her quote correct." He glanced at me and I nodded.

We were piling on and Audrey knew it. She couldn't huff and puff to get herself out of the spotlight. Resigned, she returned to the chair and sat down.

"What do you want to know?"

The Chief shrugged which immediately defused the confrontation. "I just want to know what you saw."

Audrey didn't pause to think. She just shot back an answer at him. "I don't remember. It was crazy. Chaos. People running around. Glass breaking." She sighed. "Poor Kitty. She loves those crystal glasses. I hope she can replace them."

"Let's be more specific," the Chief suggested. "What did you do when Miss Kitty looked out the window and fainted?"

Audrey looked at her hands in her lap, flicking her fingers in a nervous way. "I don't know. I-I might have just stared out the window. There was a figure, a person, out there in a black cloak. A big flowing hood shadowed the face so I couldn't see who it was. I know it sounds crazy and I know it's not possible, but..." Audrey raised her head and looked at the Chief. "... but the figure looked like the Grim Reaper."

There was a moment's silence, then the Chief asked, "Then what happened?"

Sensing that she wouldn't get much compassion or understanding from the Chief, Audrey put her tough veneer back in place and answered. "People were scrambling around like idiots. As I said, it was chaos."

"But what was happening outside?

"You mean, what was the cloaked figure doing?" The Chief nodded. "Um, I'm not sure. I think it worked its way into the woods. It was getting late and the trees were in heavy shade. The figure was in black. It all blended together." Audrey gave her head a shake, trying to clear her recollection. "The figure went into the woods and disappeared into the shadows, I think. I don't know."

The Chief gave her a hint of a smile. "That's alright. You helped a lot."

After the Chief released Audrey, it felt good to stand up.

"How much longer, Chief?" Lorraine asked.

"I think that's all for right now. I need to check with Detective Ingram, but I think y'all can head home soon."

While we waited, I slipped into the powder room for a moment's respite from all the commotion and upset that filled the rest of the house. I caught a glimpse of myself in the ornate gold-framed mirror over the sink. In all the excitement and humidity of being outside, my auburn curls had sprung out of the neat spiral bun I'd worked so hard to create for our evening out. When I stepped up to a fuchsia pink porcelain sink to dampen some of the more unruly curls, the toe of my shoe touched something on the floor. I leaned over and found a silver cufflink that looked like the same one the doctor had shown me when we'd all sat down to dinner.

Lorraine was waiting for me in the hallway. "The Chief just announced we can go home." She turned and set off for the front door, but I touched her arm to stop her.

"I have to do something first." She looked at me. "I found this on the floor of the powder room." I opened my hand to show her the cufflink with the caduceus. "I want to return it to Dr. Greene. It has great sentimental value to him."

"Wait, Abby." She lowered her voice so no one else could hear. "It would be better for you to give it to the Chief or Ingram." That advice seemed odd. "It's a murder investigation. You never know…"

I curled my fingers around the cufflink and went to find Detective Ingram. As I worked my way through the milling crowd of people, stray thoughts ran in different directions.

Is there blood on the cufflink? I hadn't inspected the piece of silver very carefully. *Could Dr. Greene be the killer? Of course not,* I argued silently. *Even if there is blood on the cufflink, it could have gotten there when he checked the body for a pulse. That's what doctors are supposed to do: Help.*

I found the detective and gave him the cufflink. I told him how I'd found it, not feeling confident that it would help.

It was such a relief to go to the front door knowing that we could all leave. There was one restriction though. The detective asked everyone to stay local for the next few days. That caused a hubbub among the visitors from out of town. It was finally resolved that Carl and Audrey would stay at the house on Tilghman Island she'd inherited from her aunt. The major parts of the renovation were done so they had all the utilities. It just wasn't up to Audrey's standard of living, as she made everyone aware.

Robert raised a furor about needing to be in the office. "I don't want to be marooned out here."

"I'm sure Harold and Kitty have internet service." Lorraine glanced at Kitty who nodded. "And I suspect you would have a room of your very own. It's just for a day or two." She pushed on as he sputtered with another objection. "I'm sure you have your laptop and/or your tablet in the car?" That stomped on his objections and he nodded silently. I guess some of my tech savvy wis finally rubbing off on her. That's what she gets for hiring a former software designer.

Harold added, "And you can borrow some of my clothes, my boy."

A flash of disgust crossed Robert's face and he held up a hand as if to stop traffic. "No, no, Harold. That's alright, I have clothes in the car." *Probably a quick change after a one-night stand.* It was a mean thought, but I suspected not far from the truth.

"So do I, but thank you," Dr. Greene added before Harold could offer his wardrobe closet. *At least the good doctor had a little more sensitivity.*

Everyone else had a local home, except Dr. Greene. I thought maybe Lorraine would invite him to stay at Fair Winds, her waterfront estate and working farm. There was certainly plenty of room, but Kitty beat her to it. She twittered what a comfort it would be to have two more strong men at the house after such a brutal attack.

After the Chief released us, no one spent time milling around for some last-minute conversation. No one, except Harold.

"May I speak to you a moment, Chief?" asked the quiet, timid man.

Lorraine rushed me out the door, but I managed to catch a glimpse of the two men entering the den off the foyer. As they closed the door, I wondered what was so private.

CHAPTER SEVEN

When a pendant is worn on a silver chain, both the pendant and chain should be cleaned often and thoroughly. Do not be surprised if a simple piece is associated with an ornate secret.

"The Butler's Guide to Fine Silver"
Mr. Hollister, 1898

Outside, Lorraine steered me toward my sweet car, the Saab 9-3 Turbo convertible. My grandmother had ordered it for herself in the custom color of teal blue, but there was nothing grandmotherly about it. The sleek lines made it look like it was racing when it was parked. And the engine was a powerhouse even without pushing the Sport button that gave it so much muscle under the hood that I almost lost control the one time I pressed it. Sadly, her terminal cancer diagnosis robbed her of the energy she needed to drive it. Still, we had many hours driving around the Pacific Northwest together with me at the wheel. Her final gift to me was the key on a ring shared with a sterling silver heart. Now, I shared the driving experience with Lorraine.

A man calling out slowed our progress. "Miss Lorraine, wait. Wait, please." Jogging over to us, the Chief caught up.

"Miss Lorraine, would you mind if I came by Fair Winds tomorrow for a few minutes?"

"Of course not, Chief. Do you want to come for lunch?"

"That would be nice, but I don't know when I can get away. Let's play it by ear, okay?"

"That would be fine. Don't even bother to call. I'll be there. What...?"

"I have to get back," and without a word of explanation, he jogged back to Kitty's house.

Lorraine and I exchanged looks and both shrugged.

"You're at the house tomorrow, aren't you Abby?"

"Yes, and I can join you at any time if you want."

"That's good. I have no idea what the Chief will want or need."

We got in the car. I didn't even think to put the convertible top down. I was so drained, it would have taken too much effort.

When we got to Fair Winds, I dropped off Lorraine at the main house and drove around to my cottage overlooking the Miles River, a valued perk of my job. There, I was met at the door by Simon, an exuberant black Lab puppy.

I'd never really wanted a dog. I figured it would be too much work and too constricting to my work hours. Writing software wasn't a nine-to-five job. My imagination and deadlines dictated when and how long I worked. The idea of stopping to take a dog for a walk, while sounding pleasant, didn't fit. But when my coworker and friend talked me into puppy-sitting while she went home to the West Coast to deal with an emergency and then never came back, Simon and I became roommates. She was gone long enough for me to figure out his schedule and for him to steal my heart. Now, I couldn't imagine life without him... and I didn't want to try. Tonight, as if he sensed that the evening hadn't gone as planned, Simon was grateful for a quick outside visit, a few doggie cookies and a slow climb up the stairs to bed.

The next morning, as soon as the sun touched the drapes of my bedroom, Simon was ready to play. I wanted to turn over and hide under the covers, away from the sun and the puppy, but he would have none of it. I reached for my soft forest green chenille robe and followed him down the steps and to the kitchen, his nails clattering on the hardwood floors. He was back at the door with his yellow tennis ball in his mouth as I set the coffee machine to brew.

"What's this? You want to play *before* breakfast?" His tail wagged so fast, I thought it would fly off his body. With guilt about being gone so late last night, I pushed myself outside. It took only a moment for the dew to saturate my slippers. I threw the ball and he raced back with it all slobbery in his mouth until I sensed that the coffee had finished brewing.

I believed it was a gift shared by all dedicated—or addicted—coffee drinkers the world over. As I sipped the heavenly hot liquid and reveled in the calm scene of an early autumn morning, thoughts about work stacked up in my little office overtook the serenity of the moment. The inventory demands of Lorraine's silver collection had grown as I found more pieces stashed in closets and boxes. I didn't want to think about what I'd find in the huge attics of the main house. The work wouldn't get done by itself. I realized with a start that I had to accomplish more in less time. The Chief was due around noon. I had no idea if or how long this murder case would pull me from my work. Quickly, I finished my first mug of the day and headed back inside.

"Simon, you're a good boy!" He flipped over on his back, the standard plea for a tummy rub. I complied, of course. "You must have known it's going to be a very busy day and I have to cram a lot of work into a short amount of time. Thank you for getting me up..." The yawn overtook me. "NO! We'd better get going."

We played on the way to the kennel where Simon would spend the day with Lorraine's dogs. Under the watchful eye of the staff, they would run around the property, sleep, tussle and wrestle and sleep. At least that would be how Simon would spend the time until we went back to the cottage. After all, he was a puppy with short legs trying to keep up with full grown Labs and a muscular

Chesapeake Bay Retriever. Yes, he would sleep away a good part of his day.

Tucked away in an office set up on the third floor of the main house, I was making good progress on my To Do list, when Lorraine tapped on the door.

"Look what I found!"

One of the gardeners, pressed into service, hefted a heavy object covered by a heavy quilt. He placed it in the center of my desk. Lorraine unwrapped it slowly with a dramatic flair to reveal a large piece of silver. Large was an understatement. Close to four feet tall, it was designed to be the focal point or centerpiece of a formal meal. It was an architectural achievement with its multiple tiers and little hanging silver baskets.

"What do you want to do with it?" I asked, not sure where to start.

She leaned against the door jamb. "It's not the kind of thing one uses every day. Maybe we should get it appraised. If it's really special, we might loan it to the silver collection at the museum in Baltimore. Oh!" She straightened up quickly and checked her watch. "That's the other reason I came up here. The Chief called. He'll be here in a half hour. We have just enough time to grab lunch. Mrs. Clark is making us something. We can eat in the kitchen."

A little later, we brought cookies and coffee into Lorraine's library where the Chief was settling into an overstuffed love seat. His gold badge was pinned to his starched white police uniform shirt that outlined the contours of his well-developed muscles.

The Chief was reaching for a second cookie when he stopped. "Hmmm, better save some for Detective Ingram. He said he'd try to join us if he could."

"Should we wait for him?" Lorraine asked.

The Chief shook his head. "No, he wasn't sure he'd make it at all. I can relay any information to him that might prove useful."

Lorraine settled back and gazed into the depths of her coffee, not wanting to start the conversation. But, at last, she did. "Chief, what can we do to help?"

"I think we told you everything we know," I added.

"And you did a good job. Your statements were very helpful." He took a sip of his coffee, the delicate china cup and saucer looking a little out of place in his massive hands, but he managed them well. "As Ingram likes to say, a witness doesn't always know what she knows, especially in a murder investigation. I thought maybe we could review things and maybe we'll get lucky."

What a perfect opening for me to ask the one question that had been bothering me. "Could we start with why Harold wanted to talk to you privately when we were leaving last evening?"

"Oh, you caught that, did you?" He sighed and put down his empty coffee cup. "He wanted to tell me something in confidence." I drew a quick breath, ready to lobby for the need for privacy when the Chief rushed on. "But… since we're meeting to see what we can uncover that will benefit this investigation, I'll tell you."

The conflict of revealing something told in confidence appeared on his face, then his muscles relaxed. "It seems that our mild-mannered Harold, comfortable in retirement and happily married, is having a second midlife crisis."

"Mid-retirement crisis?" Lorraine offered.

"Yes, that's it." The Chief smiled. "It seems that young Gretchen, full of life, overflowing with stories about the crazy world of comics and superheroes, had stoked his … well, let's say that Harold was getting frisky."

Harold was the last person I would have pegged for an affair. Not only did he not fall into the attractive category with his receding hairline, baggy shorts and black socks he wore with sandals, I was sure Kitty would have killed him if she found out. I covered my smile with my hand, not wanting to distract the Chief from his report.

"He liked to take Gretchen for lunch at the waterfront restaurant in Oxford called Capsize."

"A funny name for a restaurant," I noted.

"Yes, but it's off the beaten track and not one of the usual places Kitty frequents."

Lorraine and I exchanged looks with the same thought about what would happen if Kitty ever suspected Harold of an indiscretion.

"According to Harold, she was always willing to join him for lunch."

"She might have felt obligated, because he and Kitty had been so generous," Lorraine suggested.

"Whatever the reason, that's the way it started. Then she accepted little gifts he offered. Nothing extravagant, not at first."

"Oh, no," Lorraine breathed.

"Oh, yes. He bought her a diamond pendant."

CHAPTER EIGHT

The ice cream fork, a newly designed piece of silver flatware, combines tines to cut, spear and lift a firm bite and a wide, shallow bowl for enjoying the softer part of a serving.

"The Butler's Guide to Fine Silver"
Mr. Hollister, 1898

"Oh, no," Lorraine repeated. "He bought her a diamond pendant."

"Why didn't she just pawn the necklace and use the money?" I asked.

Lorraine gave her head a little shake. "No, no, it was worth so much more to have Harold on the hook."

"You're right," agreed the Chief. "Harold told me why he gave her such a gift. I hope I get it right. Remember what Kitty said about Gretchen developing a superhero for the comic book publisher?"

We both nodded.

"The character's name is Radiance and her superpower is the ability to radiate a villain," said the Chief.

"What happens to the villain?" Lorraine asked.

"He disintegrates where he stands. Sounds kinda cool."

"But how does that work?" I wanted to know.

"Something about a big buildup of energy in her body is concentrated by the diamond pendant her mother gave her before she died," the Chief explained.

Lorraine nodded slightly. "That's where the diamond pendant comes in. I'm no expert in comic book superheroes, but that sounds rather original."

"Harold came to me, because he saw how we were questioning everyone and he got nervous. Gretchen wore the necklace the last time she came to their house. Kitty noticed it, of course, and wanted to know where she got it."

"Gretchen played it coy, right?" asked Lorraine with an expression of distaste.

"Right. As Harold told it, Gretchen said it was a gift from a friend—you don't know him—and she smiled at Harold. He was afraid if we found out about the necklace, we'd figure it was a motive for murder and he wanted me to know it was an innocent flirtation."

"Innocent? With diamonds?" I stammered. "That sounds pretty serious to me, like Harold had an ulterior motive."

"Harold claimed the affair never started. He never even went to Gretchen's apartment."

"He certainly couldn't take her to his house," Lorraine huffed.

"He said they had drinks a few times in the afternoon at Foxy's on the water, where a lot of visitors and younger people like to hang out in St. Michaels. Harold and Kitty's friends don't go there, because they say it's too noisy, even though it's outside. He admitted he took her once to the old ferry pier in Claiborne. He vowed that nothing ever happened."

"But once she had the diamond, she had Harold in her clutches," Lorraine declared. "Are you thinking what I'm thinking?" She glanced at the two of us. "If sweet little innocent Gretchen could blackmail Robert..."

"She could blackmail Harold," the Chief and I said in unison.

"Does that mean that Harold is your prime suspect?" Lorraine asked in a hesitant voice that indicated she really didn't want to hear the answer.

The Chief pursed his lips. "He's such a mild-mannered guy..."

"And firmly under his wife's thumb," I observed. Seeing Lorraine's somewhat shocked expression, I went on. "Well, he is. Anybody can see that. Wait, you don't think that Kitty found out and ordered Harold to kill Gretchen, do you?"

The Chief's jaw dropped.

Lorraine rolled her eyes. "Why would she do that?"

I drummed my fingers on the arm of the chair. "She didn't want her friends to find out that her husband was cheating on her. It would hurt her social standing." I was making it up as I went along. "Her generation sees divorce as a stigma and she didn't want the disgrace."

"So, she opted for the alternative of murder? Pul-eeze, Abby."

The Chief held his index finger up in the air. "Wait a minute, Lorraine. It may not be so farfetched an idea as you may think. Several people reported hearing Harold say, 'I wish I hadn't done that.'"

Lorraine sat forward. "When did he say that?"

"Let me see." He leafed through his notebook and stopped on a page filled with scrawls. "After they found the body, after they identified the victim."

"Wasn't she wearing a mask?" I asked, trying to keep all the details straight.

The Chief nodded.

Lorraine leaned forward. "Who pulled it off?"

He checked his notes on another page. "Harold did."

"So," Lorraine sat back again in her chair. "He could have regretted unmasking the victim..."

"... or killing her." I added.

We fell silent, each lost in our own thoughts. Only the ticking of the grandfather clock in the foyer could be heard.

Then we all spoke up at the same time. We let the Chief go first.

"There was one other thing. Harold said he got a call from the girl that morning, yesterday morning, before she was killed. She said that she had a big surprise for him during their little dinner party. Something memorable was going to happen."

"She knew about the party," I said, as more of a statement than a question. "Kitty told us she called and invited her."

"But she had already made plans to scare us all out of our wits," Lorraine added.

The Chief looked a little confused. "How is that significant?"

Lorraine smoothed out the little napkin on her lap then looked up. "She appeared outside the dining room window when she knew we would all be at the table."

"She had a captive audience." I put in.

"Miss Kitty said the Grim Reaper…"

"Also known as Gretchen…" I said.

"Okay, Gretchen pointed at the windows."

The Chief dropped his chin to his chest with a grunt. He looked up with an effort to control his growing frustration, not at us, but the situation. "Who was she pointing at?"

Lorraine looked at me and I responded. "All of us."

The Chief's head jerked forward. "She was blackmailing all of you? All *nine* of you?"

"NO!" Lorraine and I sang out in a chorus.

He dragged his hand over his forehead though there was no perspiration there. "Well, that's a relief. Our investigation is beginning to show that the woman had a connection to several people at the table." He looked out the window. "Did you know that the Grim Reaper is supposed to carry a scythe?"

"That's right," Lorraine realized. "But she didn't have one, at least I didn't see one."

"No, we didn't find one at the scene. I think it's telling that the scythe is supposed to sever a person's ties to life on earth."

"Like the ties a husband has to his wife?" I suggested.

The Chief nodded.

With a huff, Lorraine said, "She made her point when she lifted that finger toward the people in the dining room."

"And those who had a something to hide took the accusation of the pointing finger to heart."

Lorraine jumped up and went to her desk. "Abby, I think you're on to something." She pulled out a pad of paper and a pen. "Let's go over it systematically."

I started thinking out loud. "She probably had *something* on only a few people at the table. The people who were caught in her web would know who was being threatened."

"That's right, Abby. For example, she had nothing on me," Lorraine said. "So, her pointing finger meant nothing. To me, it was a creepy prank."

The Chief rubbed his chin, thinking. "The people caught in her web, as you say, would have reacted differently than those who were not. Tell me what you saw. Who reacted differently?"

I shrugged. "I was too busy looking at the bizarre tableau to notice anyone else. Sorry, Chief."

The Chief's body sagged a little. "I guess that would have made it too easy."

"Let's try another approach. I've written the names of all the guests at the table." Lorraine showed us the list. "We can scratch out the names of the people who have good alibis."

"Right." The Chief pulled out his notebook. "Take off Kitty, yourself and Abby."

"That leaves six names," she said.

"Okay. We've confirmed that Lisa never left the kitchen, except to check the pantry for ingredients to put in the…" He made air quotes. "*restorative* smoothie for Kitty."

Something was nibbling at the edge of my memory. I checked out of the conversation around me. I'd seen something. It was… "That's it! That's what I saw! It was red!"

"Whoa, slow down, Abby." The Chief sat forward. "Tell me what you saw."

I paused, needing to describe what I could only see in my mind. "I saw something out among the trees."

Ever the cop, he wanted to get every detail. "First, when, exactly, did you see this?"

"After the figure disappeared and the men rushed outside… and before Robert came back to tell us Gretchen was the Grim Reaper and she was dead."

"And what exactly did you see?"

"Something red among the trees."

"Was it a light of some kind?" Lorraine asked, trying to understand.

"No, it wasn't like that. It was like something red moving through the trees. I remembered when you mentioned Lisa, because she was wearing red, a red dress."

The Chief's pencil was flying over a page in his notebook. "Could it have been Lisa running through the woods?"

"I—I don't know." It was hard giving evidence when I wasn't sure.

"Well, I'm going to have to double-check her alibi."

Lorraine looked out the large windows of her library at the sweeping view of the lush green lawns that ran down to the shoreline of the Miles River. "What could Gretchen have on Lisa?"

"Maybe she poisoned somebody," I tossed off.

The Chief's eyes met mine then he looked down and made a note. He was taking my comment seriously and I'd meant it as a joke. I felt a little stab of guilt. We were close in age and I thought we might become friends, but Lisa was always aloof. Then I realized my offhand suggestion was a logical possibility.

"That's a good starting point. Let's finish the list," said the Queen of Lists. Lorraine always said that making lists and checking off items was the only way she could manage her life and the farms she ran.

I'd lost count. "Who is left?"

"Audrey."

"My officers confirmed she was in the house, making a dent in Harold's brandy."

"Okay, scratch her name. Her husband Carl?"

"He was running around the woods along with the other men, according to reports."

"That leaves Carl, Robert, Harold and Dr. Greene on my list," Lorraine summed up.

"And maybe Lisa," the Chief said, snapping his notebook shut. "This narrows my investigation. Thank you, ladies. Ingram was right. We don't always know what we know."

After the Chief left, Lorraine and I sat together quietly, trying to process everything. I kept thinking back to that evening and the dinner that began as such a nice event. Then I realized there were problems right at the start. "Remember when you noticed that the table was unbalanced? That we had one too many men?"

"Yes, that's right."

"Lisa said that an unbalanced table was bad luck. I don't know about bad luck, but somebody at that table was certainly unbalanced."

"And that's not all that was wrong," Lorraine said with a little crooked smile. "Remember the placement of the cocktail fork?"

I started to laugh. "I saw your hand touch the cocktail fork and knew the mistake Kitty had made in setting the table. I thought it was touching that she'd brought out her silver flatware for the occasion. I wasn't sure if it was a usual thing for her to do for a dinner party or if she was trying to impress you."

"I don't know." Lorraine said. "Every time I've been there, she has set the table with her silver."

"I think we both spotted the mistake at the same time, just as we were sitting down. I wondered if you were going to say something."

Lorraine moved her hand to her chest in the same way Kitty liked to do and said in mock surprise, "Me? Say something? Do you think I'm a barbarian?"

"Well," I said with a serious tone. "If you'll remember, you were about to move the fork to its proper position in the table setting when I caught your eye and gently shook my head."

"Ah, that's true. I must be a closet barbarian," Lorraine

chuckled. "But seeing that slender fork with the three small tines on the left side of the dinner plate with all the other forks…it was almost too much."

I shrugged. "When you think about it, it makes sense to put forks with forks."

"Maybe, but I am my mother's daughter and my aunties' niece. They always set the table with valuable sterling silver pieces, the very ones you're inventorying now. Etiquette governed my world and every move at the dining table. A mistake grated like fingernails dragged down a chalkboard."

"I'm glad you've schooled me—"

"No, reminded you. Your grandmother did an excellent job in teaching you when you were young."

"You're right," I said, thinking of the conversations with her as she raised me. "I'm glad you *reminded* me about the proper placement of silver flatware. That knowledge helps as I work on your silver collections."

"The cocktail or seafood fork is as simple as it comes. It's the first utensil used at any formal or informal dinner."

"But why should it be placed at the far right of the dinner plate along with the knives and spoons for the meal?" I asked.

"I know, it's strange, but true. I have no clue. Maybe we should add that question to your research list."

I threw up my hands in self-defense. "Oh, please don't do that. It's long enough as it is."

"What do you say we eat dinner in the dining room tonight and set the table properly?"

"That's a great idea!"

"And let's have ice cream for dessert so we can use the ice cream forks."

Laughing together, we made our way to the kitchen, leaving some of the nervousness created by all the talk about murder and the killer's motivation behind.

CHAPTER NINE

Use great care to protect the luster of fine silver. Even plain water can leave spots that will dull the finish. Be sure to buff each piece carefully and completely to remove any spots or residue.

"The Butler's Guide to Fine Silver"
Mr. Hollister, 1898

The next morning, my mind was filled with the need to count the ice cream forks in the collection along with so many other pieces when Lorraine stopped me in the hallway on the way to my office.

"Good morning, Abby." Her face looked troubled. "I just got a strange phone call from the Chief."

"Did they catch the killer?"

"I don't think so. He wants us to gather at Kitty's house this afternoon at one."

"Everybody?"

"Yes."

"Why would he want us there? There's no way we could have committed the murder."

She shrugged. "I have no idea, but he wants us there at one o'clock. It should be interesting. He said Gretchen's mother will be there."

That piece of information stopped me in mid-step. "What?"

"She drove down from Philadelphia to identify the body." Lorraine paused for a moment then spoke softly. "He said she is a nurse. Even so, I can't imagine what it would be like seeing your daughter like that."

"Why is she going to this meeting of suspects?" I felt a ripple of revulsion. "Unless I'm missing something, the killer sat down to dinner with us and the killer will be right there with us today." I'd faced one killer and I never wanted to do it again. I shook my head firmly. "No, I couldn't do it. If she was my daughter, I'm not sure I could keep myself from jabbing a knife into the killer."

"That is an unnerving thought." Lorraine reached up and rubbed her right arm. "Let's hope she doesn't react that way. The Chief said that the mother has given him some new information that added a new perspective to the case."

"Did he say what it was?"

Lorraine smiled. "No, the Chief is getting cagey. He said if we want to know, we have to show up."

"This is sounding more and more like an Agatha Christie mystery."

Lorraine chuckled. "You might be right. There is one thing I do know. I don't want to miss this meeting."

"Do you want to leave after lunch?" She nodded. "I'll be ready." And I sprinted up the steps. So much work to do. Now, even less time to do it. But it was hard for me to concentrate. My thoughts strayed to questions about Gretchen's mother. What new information did she have that would affect the investigation? Did she have a secret jealous boyfriend? I wondered why Gretchen didn't live with her mother if money was so tight? Surely, living in the big city would help her make contacts in the art world. Why did she really want to go to this meeting? Why did she want to confront her daughter's killer? So many questions. I finally gave up and quit early to get ready for the meeting.

We weren't the first to arrive at Kitty's. Cars were parked all over the lawn. When we stepped inside the house, we met a wall of noise. Everyone was talking at once. But one voice caught my attention. It was one I recognized, heavily Southern and warm, but today, it had a hard edge. I moved closer to the open doorway into the study.

Kitty. "...told you, didn't I? He would find out... and now he has."

"Did you tell him?" Audrey. Her smokey voice was unmistakable. "Did you write that letter?"

"Why, what a terrible thing to say. Of course, I didn't. We've been friends for too long for me to rat you out to your husband. That might have been something we'd do in college, but we're way beyond that now."

"I know, I know. It's just that..."

"Just what?" Kitty demanded to know.

"After Carl got that letter telling him about my gambling, he checked our accounts, all of them. Or should I say the ones that are left."

"Oh, bless your heart, Audrey."

"We had the worst fight."

"Because you'd squandered all that money?" Kitty accused.

"No." Cranky now, she sniffed as she squirmed in her seat. "He wanted to know how he was going to pay off the letter writer."

"What if it was Gretchen who wrote that letter? What if he—"

HA! We were right. Blackmail.

"Did you hear something?" Audrey sounded fearful.

I must have made a noise. I moved to catch up with Lorraine, but before I got out of earshot, I heard Kitty say something before she shut the door.

"You're hearing things. I told you to wake up and fly right. After all, you're married to a pilot."

"A retired pilot... so unexciting." Audrey shot back,

Well, I thought, *Gretchen was a busy little bee. I'd uncovered the last secret. Time to find the Chief.*

I hustled out to the large patio nestled next to the house and accessed by several French doors. Planters overflowed with ferns and other greenery. Mums in gold and burgundy added a dash of color. Comfortable chairs and loveseats to accommodate everyone were placed so we'd all face toward the table where the police had set their papers and radios. The woods where it'd all happened were beyond the carefully manicured lawn. All the original guests were present, most standing around the refreshment table. Kitty was always the consummate hostess, the only one who would put out cookies and lemonade for a police event to catch a killer. There was one person I did not recognize sitting off to the side, close to the investigating team. The woman was rather nondescript. A few too many extra pounds had rounded out her figure. Her hair was cut short with middle age gray creeping in. Still, I couldn't figure out why she was there. There were a couple of other familiar faces in the crowd, too: police officers in plainclothes. Was it my imagination or were they strategically placed in case things got out of control? Did the Chief truly believe the killer was on the patio, calmly nibbling on a cookie? With a shudder, I realized he must.

I held my hand up to get the Chief's attention, but he waved me off. Quickly, I found a piece of paper in the bottom of my purse and scribbled a note:

Yes, it was all of them. Found out last secret.
Ask Carl and Audrey about letter and gambling.

Lorraine motioned me over to the empty chair beside her. I sat down as Detective Ingram came out of the house, putting his cell phone away in his pocket. I caught a glimpse of a self-satisfied expression on his face, but it was gone in an instant as he began to address the crowd.

"Ladies and gentlemen, thank you for making the time to come here this afternoon."

"Like we had a choice?" Everyone stared at Robert who looked as dark as a thundercloud.

"We are gathered on this sad occasion to identify the person who ended the life of one Gretchen Mayer." Ingram began to pace in front of the group as he talked. "I've been a homicide detective for many years. If there's one thing I've learned it's that people close to a crime know more than they realize. Our individual interviews have uncovered some interesting details. Though, I will admit that people will be people and spend a lot of time protesting their innocence or pointing a finger at someone else, the way the Grim Reaper pointed at all of you that fateful evening."

A shudder rippled through the group.

"In our continuing effort to find the truth, I've asked you to come here this afternoon. I thought that having you all walk through what happened would help, but then Chief Luken persuaded me that it might be too traumatic so close to the actual event. He believes we can accomplish what we need to do by just talking our way through it. I agree. As I call on you for information, I ask that you be as complete as possible. No detail is too trivial. Also, be aware that I will be asking you some questions along the way. Now, Chief, would you get us started and set the scene?"

The Chief stood up and joined the detective in front of the group. "I would like the people who were here that evening to stand when I call their names. I have excluded the two cooks who were working in the kitchen that night. We have been able to confirm their whereabouts at all times." He drew a slip of paper out of his pocket and read.

"Audrey and Carl Hirsch." They stood up on opposite sides of the patio. When Carl looked at her, she couldn't meet his eyes and looked away.

"Robert Chamberlain." He dragged himself up from his chair. His clothes were neat, but his sloppy posture made him look messy and screamed *I don't care.*

"Lisa Rayburn." She sprang from her chair. Like all of us, she was probably ready to get over this ordeal and back to her normal life.

"Abby Strickland." I tried very hard not to appear nervous. I hadn't done anything wrong, but being shy, I felt odd being the center of attention, especially among so many strangers.

"Lorraine Andrews." She glided to her feet, ever the graceful, elegant lady.

"Doctor James Greene." He stood slowly and flashed a brilliant smile all around. Considering the situation, it seemed out of place. This wasn't an introduction at a medical convention. It was a murder investigation.

"And Kitty and Harold Fitzgerald." Again, another couple who were seated on opposite sides of the patio, but the feeling between them was different from Audrey and Carl. Kitty wiggled her fingers in greeting at her husband and he gave her a smile, though it was small and a bit tentative.

He must be living in fear, I thought. *What would happen if Kitty found out what he'd done? Serves him right. Poor Kitty.*

CHAPTER TEN

When sadness strikes the House, mourning jewelry is often fashioned from sterling silver and woven hair of the loved one that is irreplaceable. Take the responsibility of cleaning these pieces yourself. You are the most experienced member of the staff and should preserve this memento that will be cherished for years.

"The Butler's Guide to Fine Silver"
Mr. Hollister, 1898

"There should be nine people standing," Detective Ingram said.

I think everybody in the immediate vicinity was mentally counting. We all looked a little nervous and self-conscious, even those who had been proven to be innocent of the crime. I suspected that the reason the chief had us all stand was to familiarize us with the suspects and add a little stress on the killer.

"Very good. Thank you Chief. You may all take a seat." Detective Ingram moved to place himself in the center of the people spread out on the patio. Lorraine and I were sitting on an outdoor settee with overstuffed cushions. Kitty and Harold were seated across the patio from one another.

"All right everybody, please sit down. Now, let's tell a story, a story that has an unhappy ending. As I remember, the weather was typical for late October, pleasant during the day and a little cool in the evening. Mr. and Mrs. Fitzgerald——"

That sweet southern voice interrupted him. "Oh detective, please call me Kitty."

Again, I wondered about Kitty's mental state. Was the Southern concept of the perfect hostess so ingrained that she could not, would not show any reaction to Gretchen's murder? Grief? Anger? Anything? Even the detective looked a little self-conscious, then he made a decision.

"All right. Miss Kitty and her husband invited some of their close friends for dinner that evening. Do you always have large sit-down dinner parties with people who all know each other?"

"Oh yes," Kitty answered with a decided lilt. "Not everyone may know one another when they first come to our home, but we encourage everyone to become friends."

He glanced toward the large palladium window. "I suppose it makes sense since you have a large dining room."

"Yes," Harold chimed in. "That was one of the most important requirements when we built the house."

"Detective," Robert added. "If we got everyone who is a Kitty and Harold dinner party alumnae together for one dinner, we'd have to rent an arena."

"Don't laugh," said Audrey. "They've started making plans for their 50th wedding anniversary and they may need that kind of venue."

The group erupted in gay laughter, born more from nerves than anything else, I suspected.

"That's good to know. But for this dinner, there were nine guests in all."

Kitty piped up again. "It was an unbalanced table. Somebody said it was bad luck."

"I don't know about bad luck, but somebody at the table was unbalanced," Robert added.

"Ladies and gentlemen," the detective said, trying to take control of the situation again. "If you would limit your comments to answers to my questions and relevant details, I would appreciate it." He shot Robert a pointed look. For once, Robert backed down.

"Now, to continue, I believe the main course-- a standing rib roast-- was served along with various side dishes. Next to the roast, there was a silver carving set consisting of a meat fork and a carving knife. Is that correct, Kitty?" She nodded. "But before your husband could begin carving the roast, you noticed something outside on the lawn and screamed."

Kitty raised her hand to cover her mouth as she remembered the horror she'd felt.

"Actually, you didn't see something. You saw *someone,* dressed in a black hooded cloak."

A tiny squeak was the only indication that what the detective said was correct.

"I assume that everyone at the table saw this figure outside?"
All the guests nodded in unison.

"I think the general reaction was that this person should not get away with playing such a horrible trick. So, everyone jumped up and ran outside to apprehend this person."

"Detective, that is not correct," Lisa said in what I suspected was the voice she used to issue commands in her restaurant kitchen. "Yes, I think everybody got out of their chairs, but only the men ran outside. You see, Kitty's response to seeing the figure was way over the top." She glanced at Kitty. "Sorry, dear." She turned back to Ingram. "She was screaming and then she fainted. Some of us stayed to help her. Some of us were so surprised, we just stood there trying to take it all in."

"And there was one other thing," I wanted to say since evidently no one else was going to mention it. "The figure looked like the Grim Reaper and it was pointing at us through the dining room window. I think that was the most frightening part of all."

Detective Ingram looked at the Chief and gave him a little nod. "Very good. Thank you, Ms. Strickland." He turned to Harold. "And I think that there is another detail we need to add, isn't there, Mr. Fitzgerald?"

Harold's voice cracked as he spoke. "Yes, yes detective. Before I left the dining room, I grabbed the carving knife." He looked down at his hands. "I don't know why. It must've been a natural reaction that I didn't want to go up against a crazy person without some kind of weapon for protection. If I had known what was going to happen…" His words faded.

Ingram clasped his hands behind his back and gave Harold a half smile. "I think it was a natural reaction. Do you own a gun?"

Harold cast a furtive glance at his wife and looked away immediately. "What does that have to do with anything?"

"No, detective we do not own a gun," said Kitty matter-of-factly.

Harold mumbled something. The detective asked him to repeat what he said. And our host raised his head high and said defiantly, "Yes, detective. I own a gun that is legally registered and I keep it locked up here in the house."

Kitty gasped. "Harold!" She jumped up from her chair and an officer quietly moved closer to her, just in case. "You told me you sold it after I said how uncomfortable it made me feel."

Kitty, I thought, *I suspect there is a lot more that you don't know about Harold.*

"You can have that discussion with your husband later. Perhaps he will tell you what I consider a possible motive."

"WHAT?" Kitty screeched. "I demand to know what you mean."

Detective Ingram was certainly stirring up emotions and in front of everyone. It was a little risky and unfair, but I was curious what would come to the surface.

Harold raised his shoulders and let them fall in a dramatic shrug. "We had drinks, that's all. Only a few times." Finally, he got the courage to meet Kitty's eyes and seeing the hurt there, he rushed to explain. "Nothing happened."

Kitty sank to her chair. "You were having an affair!" she whimpered. "With that *girl?*"

"No, never. Nothing happened," he pleaded for her to believe him.

The detective cleared his throat. "Perhaps you could talk about it later." Harold sank into himself. Kitty dabbed the corner of her eye while the detective walked slowly, casually around the group.

"Now, let's continue with what was happening in the house. I believe, Audrey, that you went to get the brandy to help revive Kitty. Is that correct?"

"I got the brandy for Kitty, sure, but also for myself. Seeing that horrible creature outside pointing at all of us will be in my nightmares for a long time. I think I was more in need of a shot or two than Kitty was."

"So, you left the dining room alone. Is that correct?"

"Yes."

"I'm curious, how did you know where to find the brandy?"

"Kitty and I are old friends from college. I've spent many, many hours in this house. On more than one occasion, we have sat in the study having a brandy. It's kept on a sideboard in that room."

"Good. Thank you, Mrs. Hirsch."

The Chief motioned for the detective's attention and added, "We have established in our investigation that she was not gone long enough to commit the crime outside."

"Good. Thank you, Chief." He began to walk again. "So, about that time, Kitty was reacting to what she had seen and was in the dining room with Lorraine, Abby and Lisa while Audrey was getting the brandy." As he casually walked through the group, he had positioned himself in front of Lisa. "And then I believe you left the room."

"Yes, I did. Brandy is fine, but in an emergency, the body needs something restorative. I am an expert in food and its nutritional values. I went to the kitchen to make Kitty a restorative smoothie to help her body recover from the shock. The cook saw me there and can vouch for me," she said confidently.

"I believe you were wearing a red dress that evening."

"That's right," she said, her confidence a little shaken by his focus on what she wore.

"And you say that you didn't leave the kitchen?" The detective continued.

"Yes. No, that's wrong. I went into the pantry, the little room off the kitchen to look for possible ingredients for the smoothie."

"And you were the only one wearing red that evening, correct?"

"Yes, yes that's right." She answered as she looked at the other guests seated around the patio as if to confirm her answer.

"Then why did Abby see a flash of red moving through the trees outside?" The blood drained from Lisa's face. "The way she described it in her statement was… Chief, could you read that section for me please?"

The Chief leafed through some papers and pulled out a sheet. "'I saw something red moving in the woods. It wasn't a light. It looked like a piece of clothing that somebody had on. It was hard to tell what it was and I couldn't see who it was. It just appeared, moving between the trees.' That's the end of that section."

"How do you explain that, Lisa?"

"I-I can't," she stammered. "It wasn't me. I was in the kitchen and the pantry making a smoothie for Kitty."

The detective kept his eyes on the woman, intrigued. "Did you know that it was Gretchen who was dressed up as the Grim Reaper?" Lisa met his gaze and shook her head. He frowned a little. "Miss Rayburn, did you know the deceased?"

Her eyes fell to her hands clasped tightly in her lap. Barely above a whisper, she said "Yes."

Detective Ingram stood in front of Lisa with his legs spread apart and his arms folded across his chest. "And how did you know the deceased?"

"She worked as a dishwasher in a restaurant over in Baltimore where I was a sous chef early in my career."

"And what happened, because something did happen, didn't it, Ms. Rayburn?"

Slowly, she nodded. "We were very busy one night. We were slammed. We were running out of the crab special and I hadn't alerted the chef or the house manager. It was my job and we only needed one more order. I-I used a leftover crab that was iffy and the diner got very sick and was taken to the hospital. During all the commotion, Gretchen came over to me and said that she had seen what I had done. She said if I made it worth her while, she wouldn't say anything. I was stunned. This dishwasher, this nobody was trying to blackmail me! I told her no, absolutely not. She marched right over to the chef and told him what happened. I'll never forget her malicious smile. Fortunately, the diner recovered by the next morning, but I lost my job. I was on a fast track to get my own kitchen and it's taken me a long time to claw my way back."

"And you resented her." Ingram made it a declaration. "She almost cost you your career."

"No, she didn't."

The detective kept hammering away. "You hated her."

"It was my fault." She raised her eyes to Ingram. "It was no one's fault but mine…and something I would never do again. If you'd asked me that night if I wanted her dead, I might've said yes. But she taught me an important lesson and now, I'm doing what I love right here in St. Michaels. It might even be sweeter, because of that night. I learned that what you achieve is important, but how you achieve it is the most important thing of all."

Detective Ingram gave his head a sharp nod, dropped his arms and began to walk again.

Another suspect down, but still more to go to find the killer.

CHAPTER ELEVEN

A napkin ring is often associated with a particular member or friend of the family. It may be engraved with the birth or christening date of the person and often given as a gift on that occasion. Two napkin rings are given when there is a family wedding or a silver wedding anniversary.

"The Butler's Guide to Fine Silver"
Mr. Hollister, 1898

"This is ridiculous." Robert jumped to his feet. "I have better things to do with my time."

As he took a step away, Ingram's voice froze him to the spot. "Mr. Chamberlain." The detective enunciated each syllable distinctly. "Mr. Chamberlain, Sit. Down."

Robert turned and looked over his shoulder at the man in charge of the investigation. "Why—"

"Why should you care?" Ingram rushed to complete his question. "Because a young woman had her life stolen from her way before her time. And if that isn't a good enough reason, Mr.

Chamberlain, because I know you are a suspect and why. An educated man like you should have realized that a little careless pillow talk could get you into a lot of trouble down the road. Now, unless you want me to enumerate that information, I suggest that you do as you're told. Sit. Down."

A low-level murmur passed through the group. I watched as people speculated about what Robert had done. Could they also be worried that the detective knew any of their innermost secrets? Detective Ingram had certainly planted unease and suspicion very well among those gathered on the patio. He let them whisper for a few moments while he wandered among the group.

When he sensed they had run out of flimsy theories and guesses, he stopped and turned on Carl. The quick movement snagged everyone's attention.

"Mr. Hirsch, would you please tell me why the victim was blackmailing you and your wife?"

I was sure that Carl was going to drop the glass of lemonade in his hand. "What?!" He choked. "I don't think—"

The detective turned and walked away towards the edge of the patio to take in the view, his back to the group. "Come on now, Mr. Hirsch. Gretchen was a busy girl. Probably unbeknownst to you she was busy blackmailing several people who are sitting on this patio. I just assume you and your wife were also a target." He turned and his eyes bore into Carl. "So, why don't you tell me what Gretchen had on you?"

"How did you know about the letter?" Carl said just above a whisper as his military erect posture collapsed.

"Don't you dare, Carl," Audrey hissed from where she sat several feet away from her husband. "Don't you dare say another word."

He raised his head and turned to her. The sadness on his face had added age lines right in front of our eyes. "I have to, Audrey. You have an alibi. You never went outside. You're in the clear. But he's thinking I might be the killer? I'm willing to give up money for you, Audrey, but I'm not willing to go to prison." He stood up, threw his shoulders back, raised his chin and stopped just short of saluting. "Detective, I am married to a woman addicted to gambling. I've had my suspicions for a while. Being a military wife, left at home, is not easy… and it can be boring. She finally admitted it to me last week. She has squandered huge amounts of our money and has bent the terms of her inheritance from her aunt just enough that it might be criminal. That little…" Carl squeezed his eyes shut, trying to regain control, and began again. "That girl sent my wife a threatening letter making accusations about her gambling debts. She threatened Audrey that she'd tell me and everybody we know unless she made a …" Carl made air quotes "small monetary contribution to her." Carl directed his steely gaze at the detective. "It was sheer blackmail."

He took a deep breath and spoke without the angry edge to his voice. "There was no way my wife could pay her off. Fortunately, she came to me with the truth and the letter. At least we still have enough of a relationship for her to lean on me. I'm grateful for that." He walked over to where Audrey was sitting and looked around at everyone. "There! Now, you all know our sordid little secret." His eyes swept the group again with an attitude that challenged anyone to make a comment. No one did. He looked back at the detective who, with a silent nod, gave him permission to sit down next to his wife.

Detective Ingram moved to the front of the group and grasped his hands behind his back. "This is a baffling case. On a pleasant fall evening, nine people sat together to enjoy a delicious dinner served with the elegance of fine china, lead crystal glasses and sterling silver flatware. Nine people who see a figure outside dressed as the Grim Reaper who points her finger at them all. Pandemonium — born of shock, dread and yes, guilt — breaks out. It isn't long before the Grim Reaper is found dead and is unmasked.

"Gretchen Mayer. A young woman steeped in the comic book world and superhero culture. A talented artist and storyteller who was about to break through with her own heroine. Also, a woman who had found ways to control and threaten others. That evening, she dressed in a dramatic black cloak, stood outside this lovely home and pointed at someone…" Ingram held up his index finger. "No, that's not right. She wasn't pointing at just one person; she was pointing at everyone in the dining room. That's the way it seemed to me at the beginning of this investigation. Nine people. Nine suspects."

There was a general shuffling among the group. Nerves finally overwhelmed people's calm, detached demeanor.

"As my colleagues and I did what we were trained to do to investigate, we began to discover some truths, some small, some major. We soon established that three people had solid alibis." With each name he pointed to the individual in the group. "And they were Lorraine Andrews, Abby Strickland and the hostess Kitty Fitzgerald. Now, we were down to six suspects, and of those, two left the dining room, but did not leave the house. Now, we are down to four suspects, but there's one troubling point. Abby Strickland believes she saw a flash of red moving through the woods. Only one of those suspects, Lisa Redburn, was wearing red that evening. Did she leave the house? As you all heard, Lisa's career was almost destroyed by the victim." He shrugged. "No, at that moment in time, I would say that Gretchen destroyed Lisa's career. She was fired from a job she loved. She had to reestablish herself by starting all over again to prove that she could be trusted to prepare safe meals for restaurant patrons."

Lisa sprang to her feet and declared, "I told you, I did not leave the house. I did not hurt or kill that girl." In defiance, she bounced down on her chair and crossed her legs.

"Yes, you did, but for the moment, I believe we are back up to five suspects."

Lisa huffed in disgust.

"Yes, we still have Lisa." Ingram turned a little to look at his next suspect. "And we have Robert who disclosed a secret during pillow talk." His eyes found the next suspect. "Carl who had received a threatening letter." Slowly, Ingram turned his head until his gaze fell upon the small, timid man whose forehead was beaded with sweat. "And Mr. Fitzgerald," he said almost soothingly. "Sir, would you tell us please why you said, 'I wish I hadn't done that.'"

"No, I didn't say that." His voice was strained with desperation.

Robert called out. "Harold, it's time to confess."

On the other side of the patio, Kitty gasped. People leaned closer, not wanting to miss a word of his confession, the man who took the carving knife from the dinner table and dashed outside. Did he really thrust it into the poor girl's chest?

"Harold, why did you say that you wish you hadn't done that?"

The little man let out a deep sigh that made his body look like a deflated balloon. "I said that because there were so many things I wish I hadn't done. I wish I hadn't knelt down and removed the mask. I wish I had never seen her sweet face contorted in shock and pain. I see it all the time now in my daydreams and nightmares. I wish I hadn't seen the diamond pendant she wore around her neck, the neck that was now splattered with her blood. I wish I had never given it to her."

"What! You gave Gretchen that diamond pendant?" His wife Kitty demanded to know.

"It was a gift, an innocent gift to celebrate her creativity and her success at getting the attention of her publisher. Her dream was about to become a reality. She didn't have a friend who could mark the occasion like I could."

"And what else did you do, Harold?" Kitty snarled. Her face looked like it was chiseled from ice.

Harold whipped around to face his wife. "I didn't do anything, Kitty."

"Except give a pretty young woman a diamond necklace. What a stupid old man you are."

He stood a little taller. "Old, definitely. Stupid, probably. But at least she appreciated the gesture." He took in a deep breath and continued. "At least she appreciated the attention in the beginning. But then she said she needed more money to tide her over until the publisher bought her superheroes story. I explained to her that we had decided we had given her enough money. That's when she threatened to tell you, Kitty, tell you everything." Harold turned his attention back to the detective. "And I suppose that makes me a prime suspect in your eyes. I will admit that I thought she was sweet in the beginning. I enjoyed spending time with her and doing little things for her. I will tell you that I resented her threat after all my wife and I had done for her. But, detective, I did not kill her." His eyes fell on every one of his friends and guests who were sitting there listening to his confession as he repeated the words, "I did not kill her."

But Harold wasn't done. "I know it probably sounds lame now, but something happened in the woods while we were searching for the dark figure. I was running along with the carving knife in my hand—probably not a smart thing to do—when somebody came up from behind and crashed into me. I was knocked to the ground. I even got dirt all over my new pants." Harold was frantic, desperate to be believed. "I must have let go of the knife and spread out my hands to cushion my body from hitting the ground hard. A man of my age can't afford a fall. I heard the other men yelling and I climbed back to my feet and ran to meet up with them. I didn't have the knife. I don't think I even saw it on the ground. Whoever slammed into me must've taken it."

"Did you see who it was?" asked the detective.

"No, I was hit from behind. The only thing I saw close-up was the ground. I'm sorry." He sat down and looked like a great weight was off his shoulders.

"Now, we have identified the four people at the table that evening who had a motive—" Lisa started to protest when Ingram held up his hand for her to stop. "... who had a possible motive for killing Gretchen."

I leaned over to Lorraine and whispered. "Four? There are *five* people left."

As if Ingram heard me, he amended his comment. "We've identified all the people at the dinner table that evening with a credible motive for committing murder... except one."

CHAPTER TWELVE

*Use of a Baptismal Shell or Christening Shell is a tradition dating
back to ancient times. Some of the earliest religious artwork depicts
baptism by pouring water from a scallop shell. Though used rarely, it is
a valued piece passed down from one generation to another. It must be
in pristine condition when it is needed for the rite.*

"The Butler's Guide to Fine Silver"
Mr. Hollister, 1898

"It would not be fair to leave out the good Dr. Greene." Ingram
gave the man a wide smile. "It's almost an insult to suggest that
a doctor would kill when he's sworn an oath to *Do no harm*. But I
want to be fair to everyone."

"Why would I be interested in fairness, detective?" The doctor
gave the detective a tight smile that didn't reach his eyes. "I just
want to leave."

Ingram returned the false smile. "I think you share that feeling
with everyone here. You'll be on your way shortly, but indulge me
for now." He didn't wait for a response as he resumed his casual

walk around the group. "You may not realize it, but it would take a lot of time and effort to gather information about a doctor. There's not a number I can call to say, 'Give me everything you have on Doctor So-and-So.' It doesn't work that way. Imagine my surprise when a prime source of information walked into my office." He gestured toward a woman sitting at the far edge of the patio with her back to the group. "This is Elizabeth Mayer." She rose and stood beside him. "She is Gretchen's mother...and a nurse," he added with extra weight in his tone.

It was the woman I'd noticed earlier. I got the impression that as a nurse, she had always focused her attention on her patients, not herself. As Ingram let the gasps of surprise and mumblings die down, she scanned the group until her eyes fell on Dr. Greene.

She spoke directly to him as if the rest of us had melted away. "Of course, my name wasn't Mayer back when you were in medical school. It was Mrs. Cooper." She paused to let the information sink in.

"Beth?"

Everyone's eyes went to the doctor and saw the moment he made the connection.

"Beth, is that you?"

"Yes, Jimmy, though I understand you go by James now. You started using the more formal name in your last year. You said it sounded more proper, commanded respect and you've done quite well for yourself."

"Oh, Beth, I had no idea Gretchen is, was your daughter. I'm so sorry."

"Thank you, James. It's ironic that she should die twice before she turned thirty and you should be around both times."

"Would you care to explain, Ms. Mayer?" suggested Ingram.

She smoothed her deep gray shirtwaist dress, stood with her shoulders back and raised her chin high as she braced herself to face off with the illustrious doctor. "I met Jimmy Greene when he was in his third year of medical school and I was a nurse in the teaching hospital. We shared something more than our mutual love of medicine. We shared a desperate need for money. His parents had announced that they were getting a divorce and he said it was going to be very messy. Back then, messy equaled expensive. They had told him that they didn't have enough money to pay his tuition for his last year in school. They told him he was ingenious and they were sure he would come up with a good alternative.

"We met one night in the empty hospital cafeteria. The kitchens were closed but somebody kept the coffee urn full. I was sitting at a table in the corner, worrying about what I was going to do. I had married a man who I thought loved me. We had a couple of happy years and then I guess he got bored. Before I knew it, he announced he was leaving me and wished me luck in figuring out how I was going to pay the bills he had run up on our joint credit card accounts. Oh yes, he had cleaned out every bank account he could. I didn't even have enough money to hire a lawyer.

"Then you, Jimmy, walked up and said, 'You look like you need a friend. May I sit down?' And that was either the best or the worst moment of my life. I'm not proud to admit it," she glanced at Ingram. "But I understand that the Statute of Limitations has run out so I don't have to hold anything back. We talked for a while and you evidently felt comfortable in laying out your scheme that would help us both. Abortions were legal in that state. But not late term abortions. You said that a couple of women had asked you for help in terminating their pregnancies… and they were willing to pay. You said that the women were so desperate that if we wouldn't do the procedure, they would either find someone else or do something that might endanger their own lives. You made it sound easy. You had the patients. You had the place with the equipment we needed and it was close to the hospital in case something went wrong. But you needed a nurse. With just a nod of my head, my whole life changed." One of the female police officers brought her a glass of water and she drank deeply.

I glanced around the room to gauge the response of the people. Some looked stunned. Some looked disgusted.

Dr. Greene jumped to his feet. "This is outrageous! Lies! Nothing but lies!"

"Please sit down, Dr. Greene," Ingram said calmly. "You'll have time to speak, if you wish." He turned to Ms. Mayer. "Please continue."

"You were right about two things. The women were truly desperate and would have terminated their pregnancies with or without our help. And you were right that they would pay serious money. After just three procedures, I was back on my feet and had a lawyer working on my behalf who could protect me and get rid of the scumbag who was my husband. You were able to pay your tuition and fees and were on track for graduation with honors. I thought we were done.

"One day, you came to me and asked for my help one more time. I didn't want to do it. My conscience had caught up with me and I wanted to forget everything we had done. You told me the story of this poor girl who had been raped and kept silent. When she finally admitted to herself that she was pregnant, it was no longer possible for her to have a legal abortion. You played on my sympathies. You talked about how her life would be ruined forever. You talked about what kind of a life this baby would have in the care of a teenage girl, because no one would want to adopt a baby conceived in rape. I finally agreed. But I was shocked when she walked into our little examination room where we did the procedure. She was definitely late in her term.

"When I told you, I didn't want to do the procedure, you threatened me. You said if I didn't help this one last time, you would tell the nursing administrator what I had done, that I had done the procedures on the three other women. I didn't know what to do. I was faced with a very real threat that would end my career, a career I loved, and might even land me in jail. You were willing to do the procedure. The girl had come with money, a lot of money. Obviously, someone wanted this baby gone. It didn't help that she sat in front of me sobbing, begging for my help. It wasn't about money anymore. It was about sanity.

"I finally agreed and you took the baby. You ordered me to

take *it* out of the room so the girl couldn't see it. You ordered me to *dispose of it.* I don't think you wanted to see it either because it was fully formed."

Dr. Greene was on his feet again, yelling. "Lies! All lies!" He stomped over to the door where he was stopped by an officer in plainclothes.

"No, doctor. I think you need to sit down and hear the rest of the story." Reluctantly the man took a seat. "Now, Ms. Mayer, please finish your story."

"I did as you asked. I took the baby out of the room and I never went back. Why? With all the odds against her, she started to breathe."

Many in the group gasped.

"I got her support. I got her the help she needed. And when she could thrive on her own, I moved us to a city where no one knew me.

"I went back to my maiden name and made up a dead husband. I got a job at the local hospital. They were thrilled to have someone with my experience. There was no shortage of people to watch over her while I was at work. My baby got a second chance at life. She thrived. We never had a lot of money. I couldn't always give her what I wanted or what she deserved. She grew into a smart, talented, creative young woman. I did my best, but when it came to college, we faced the grim reality of college loans. She was always so optimistic. She was so confident that if she studied hard in her classes, she would get her big break and be able to pay them off." She chuckled a little. "She even talked about how she was going to take care of me. Buy me a fancy condo when we moved to a big city like New York or Los Angeles. Big dreams. While she got a job, a good job, in her profession, the money was always tight. It was the loan payments that almost did her in. She got offers of employment that paid better, but they were outside of her chosen field. She wanted to hold on a little while longer. She was so sure that it would all work out.

"She came to me one day in tears. She had missed several payments and they were going to go after her salary. She was so afraid that if her boss found out, he would fire her. She didn't need much, but it was more than I had to give her. She laid out a scheme to bridge the gap. It was all my fault."

The woman started to cry. "Several years earlier, she badgered me for information about her real mom, because she knew she was adopted. She wanted to know about her dad. She was like any other adopted child who wanted to know where she came from. In a weak moment, I told her the truth. Now, she was going to use that truth. Not by going after her biological parents. Her target was you, Jimmy. She had uncovered your identity – I told you she was smart – and tracked you down. She was going to pay you a visit, the illustrious Dr. James Greene. She said she was going to demand money from you or she would ruin your career the way that you had almost ruined her life."

CHAPTER THIRTEEN

Pieces of jewelry or ornamentation worn by men possibly require more vigilance than those worn by the ladies and girls of the House. Many pieces of his wardrobe are made of wool. No matter the high quality of the wool fabric, the oils that occur naturally can have a devastating effect on sterling silver, even causing permanent damage.

"The Butler's Guide to Fine Silver"
Mr. Hollister, 1898

The mother of the murdered young woman wiped her tear-streaked face. "I told Gretchen not to contact you. I begged her. I said we'd find the money some other way." She shredded the damp tissue the way people do when they're upset. "I said she was smart, but she did have trouble sometimes with the line between right and wrong."

Her eyes hardened. She raised her chin. "That afternoon, I knew that if she threatened you, you would do anything to stop her. I know you have always been capable of doing *anything* to get what you want. You did it the day Gretchen was born, or should I say, the day I saved her life. The day you ordered me to *dispose* of her. And I am sure that you did whatever you thought you had to do to stop her from exposing you and ruining your precious reputation." A single tear escaped from an eye and trickled down her cheek. "That afternoon when I told her not to contact you, that was the last day I saw my daughter alive. You killed her!" She lunged toward the doctor. The Chief caught her around the shoulders to stop her, but he couldn't stop the words she cried. "You killed her! I know it by all that is holy."

The Chief with the help of the female officer hustled the distraught mother into the house. "Murderer. Murderer!" The words bounced off the trees where Gretchen was killed.

I felt like I'd been body-slammed by all the emotions flooding from the nurse, now mother of a dead child she'd saved from extinction. I couldn't turn and meet Lorraine's eyes. I'd almost bullied her to come for what should have been a relaxing social evening. Now, we were exposed to the reality of hurt, anger and accusation. Lorraine reached out and covered my hand with her own and squeezed. Somehow, she understood and forgave me.

Ingram saw that every eye was either boring into the accused doctor or staring at him then looking away in disgust. "Ladies and gentlemen, quiet down. Dr. Greene, do you have anything to say in response?"

Dr. Green looked back at the detective with a vacant expression. He crossed his legs in a slow, casual manner. Then he laughed. Laughed so loud it reverberated through the lovely area surrounding Kitty's house. Not one other person laughed or even smiled in sympathy with the doctor. He noticed it, too. His laughter petered out. He took a different approach.

Jumping up from his chair, he announced in his most commanding voice. "That is the most outrageous story I've ever heard. I'm a prominent and highly respected physician. You said it yourself, detective. I'm dedicated to saving lives, not taking them."

Lisa, who sat in the chair next to him, got up and moved.

"Oh, come on. You all know me. You know the kind of man I am. Helping people when they need it." His eyes swung around the room. Was he looking for support? Finding none, he focused on one person. "Lisa, you trust me. Who did you call when the hot oil burned your arm? You didn't think to go to the emergency room first. You called me. ME!" He paused to let his words sink in. When she gave no response, he bellowed. "You can't honestly believe these groundless accusations! Why would I do such a thing?" He turned his head back to the detective. "You can't believe that woman."

Ingram pursed his lips. "You know, that was my first reaction. Sure, if something goes wrong in a hospital, the doctor is often the first one blamed. Away from the hospital, doctors have a solid reputation for being caring, knowledgeable... a pillar of the community."

Feeling vindicated, Dr. Greene folded his arms and gave him a smile that had not an ounce of warmth or delight.

"But..." Ingram gave a deep sigh. "then I did what homicide detectives are supposed to do. I followed, as the British say, the line of inquiry. The hospital confirmed that both you and Mrs. Mayer were there at the same time. The medical school administration was kind to go back in their records to find the tuition check payments for your schooling. The first three years were paid with checks signed by your father. The last year, you were the one who signed the check."

"My father must have put the money in my account," he said with a little chuckle. "I don't really remember."

"It doesn't matter. We are checking it out. It will take some time, but I think it will be worth it. Then I think we'll be able to jog your memory."

"Whatever for? It was a long time ago."

"If Ms. Mayer is to be believed, it is highly relevant to this case... and the naming of the killer."

Dr. Greene dropped his arms and stood straight. "I resent that, Detective." He sneered. "I have better things to do than to wait around while you try to concoct evidence against me, evidence that isn't there." He stood up and adjusted the collar of his polo shirt so it stood up a little bit in the back. "Now, if you'll excuse me. I have important matters that need my attention." He turned to Kitty. "Thank you for your hospitality. I really have to pack and get on my way. I'll call you next week."

He headed for the door into the house, but it was suddenly blocked by a St. Michaels police officer who answered a silent question from Ingram. "Yes, sir."

"Positive?"

"Yes, sir."

Irritated, the doctor looked up at the sky. "More games, detective? Well, have fun." He turned to leave, but Ingram's words stopped him.

"Tell me, are you right- or left-handed?" Ingram was casual, unperturbed.

"What does that have to do with anything?"

"Humor me." There was nothing humorous in his expression.

The doctor stepped back toward the center of the gathering to face Ingram. "I'm left-handed, if you must know." He looked around the group. "I suppose he's going to make some joke about being a southpaw and how that proves I'm a killer."

He flashed a big smile at Ingram. It was a challenge, a gauntlet thrown down at Ingram's feet, *Go ahead, do your worst.*

"And if you checked for a pulse, you would probably do it with your left hand?"

"Yes, I suppose so. Yes." The doctor shook his head. "I don't know where you're going with this. You sound very sure of yourself."

Ingram stepped forward and held out something in the palm of his hand to the doctor. "Is this yours?"

People strained to see what it was. Whispers began from people seated closest so soon all knew what it was. Of course, when I saw the glint off the silver, I knew. It was the cufflink.

"Oh good, you found it. I thought I'd lost it." The doctor reached for it, but Ingram rolled up his fingers into a fist and withdrew it. "It's mine and I'd like to have it back," the doctor insisted.

"I'm afraid that's not possible right now. It's evidence."

"What? Don't be ridiculous," the doctor shot back.

"I'm afraid it's true. While we've been chatting out here on this delightful patio, a search warrant was executed on this house."

The doctor's head pivoted back and forth between Harold and Kitty. Finally, it was his hostess who nodded solemnly.

"Actually, not the whole house. Just the guest room. *Your* room."

"You have no right to go through my things," he breathed in barely suppressed anger.

"Yes, I'm afraid the judge gave us that authority. And look what we found. Officer?"

The officer in the doorway held up the other cufflink. The doctor lunged for it, but the officer reacted quickly and delivered the mate to Ingram.

"At least you know that both cufflinks are safe."

"Give them to me," the doctor demanded.

Ingram ignored him as if he hadn't spoken. "And they share a little secret."

The people were so silent and intent on what was happening that when the geese flew overhead and honked, we all jumped.

"The secret is they both have blood on them. Blood that matches the victim, Gretchen Mayer."

"That's impossible. I just checked for a pulse with my left hand, like you said. Any blood would only be on the left one."

Ingram gazed into the woods. "That would be true, if that's all you did. But the medical examiner thinks you tried to withdraw the knife. He thought it was a precise thrust, suggesting the killer knew exactly where to strike." Ingram turned to face the doctor with an expression of curiosity. "Or did you panic? After all, you're used to saving lives, not taking them. Did you try to pull the knife out so you could stab her again? To make sure she was dead?" The doctor just stared at him, his jaw slack. "But you were right. The first stab was a little bit off the mark. The tip lodged in a bone. When you couldn't slide the blade out again with one hand, you used both hands, exposing your right cufflink to the last drops of blood pumped out of the body. You still couldn't budge it, so you left it there and ran into the woods when you heard the men approaching." Ingram shook his head a little. "You really shouldn't have knocked Harold to the ground. He's an old man." There was the beginning of a protest from Harold, but Ingram ignored it. "His bones are getting brittle. You could have caused him real injury. Not good, Doctor."

The doctor made a dash for it. Someone stuck out his leg and tripped the doctor who ended up flat on his face. Officers put their hands on him and hustled him away.

"I always wanted to do that," Robert said while rubbing his leg. "But I didn't think it would hurt so much."

Everyone burst out in laughter, a relief after such horrible revelations. Then those sounds of merriment petered out and people acted embarrassed. The police hustled Dr. Greene away. The other guests were reluctant to leave. Some got up to refill their coffee cups. Others shifted chairs so they could chat, trying to process the developments.

Someone was heard to say, "It's too bad Gretchen lost her life."

Kitty turned toward her and responded, "That's the way the cookie crumbles."

"Kitten, that's a little harsh," Harold mewed.

She turned her head slowly in his direction and rocked her head back a little, one eye almost squeezed shut, her mouth drawn into a curious line. "Knowing what I know now, you have no idea what harsh is, my sweet." The sarcasm dripped from her last two words. "And don't call me Kitty or Kitten. You've lost that privilege. It's Esther to you from now on."

With her head held high, her steps firm and her chin leading the way, she floated out of the room. I caught a glimpse of Harold – his head hanging low, his shoulders slumped – before he escaped to a path into the woods, unwilling to face his guests. The winner in the tussle of what they call marriage was obvious. Or as Kitty would say, *Crystal Clear.*

CHAPTER FOURTEEN

*The Five O'Clock Tea Spoon harkens back to the era when tea was
served at that time. It is slightly shorter than a teaspoon and slightly
larger than an after-dinner coffee spoon.*

"The Butler's Guide to Fine Silver"
Mr. Hollister, 1898

A couple of days later, the Chief and Detective Ingram made themselves comfortable in Lorraine's study at Fair Winds. Two walls of windows overlooked lush green lawns that ran to the Miles River below. Bookshelves covered the other walls except where an exquisite marble fireplace presided over the room. A heavy mahogany library table with carved legs served as Lorraine's desk where she managed the details of Fair Winds farm and social activities.

We settled with our coffee along with some of those amazing donuts the cook, Mrs. Clark, made with a little specialty machine. It turned out a fresh donut every three minutes. Hot, delicious and worth the wait.

The silence was finally broken by Lorraine. "We've spent some unhappy moments in this room, haven't we?"

Ingram nodded. "Are you sure you want…" His voice trailed off.

"… to talk about another murder?"

He looked down at his coffee. I too noticed the pain in Lorraine's eyes and looked away.

Lorraine continued. "At least this time, it didn't have a direct impact on my home."

I glanced over at her quickly. I knew she was referring to Evie's murder. Was that all? I looked away and said nothing. I realized that enough time hadn't passed yet to resume a normal life.

"I don't think anyone will ever forget that dinner party at Kitty's," Lorraine said softly.

The Chief sat back. "I must say that this has been one of the shortest murder investigations of my career."

"Didn't I tell you in the beginning," I said with a big smile. "That this case was tied up with a big bow?"

He chuckled quietly. "Yes, yes, you did."

Lorraine gazed out a large window and spoke as if she was thinking out loud. "I find it shocking what people will do when they don't have the money they need. I guess I shouldn't be surprised."

"Unfortunately, we see the results too often," Ingram remarked.

"But blackmail? It took a lot of effort on her part to dig up dirt on so many people and then to have the nerve to confront them." She shook her head.

"It's a messy business, but blackmail is extortion, plain and simple. It's punishable as a criminal act in every state and on the federal level." Ingram explained.

"You're right," the Chief said. "I can see why she did it and threatened her marks, the people she was blackmailing, when they were all together at the dinner. Harold told me that she'd given him a short deadline. She had the chance to change her life, but she needed a chunk of money to take care of her bills so she could concentrate on her art. She spread her want among several people to make sure she got the money she needed." He sighed. "And it cost her."

"And Radiance, her superhero, has lost her creator," Lorraine added.

"I heard a rumor," I offered, wanting to shift the conversation away from such gloomy thoughts. "Kitty is thinking about moving away. She feels there is a real ghost there now."

Lorraine reached for her donut. "I'm sure that's just talk, at least I hope so. When she realizes how special she's become, how unique to have survived the pointing finger of the Grim Reaper, how everybody will want to see the place and hear the story, she'll change her mind."

"I'm afraid you're right," said Ingram. "People have a morbid curiosity. She'll be a very popular hostess for a long time."

"I understand you can't get a table at Lisa's restaurant in town," I commented. "Everybody wants to get close to notoriety."

Lorraine tilted her head to the side a little and made a *hmmm* noise.

"I know that look. What are you thinking?" I asked.

"What? Oh. I was just thinking it's ironic that it was Harold's idea to have that little dinner party to tell scary stories."

"That's right." I turned to the two law enforcement officers. "I don't know if your investigation picked up that detail. Harold wanted to rid Kitty of her nightmares. Scary stories from Halloween would upset her sleep and his for weeks."

The Chief chuckled a little. "And he ended up with the worst kind of scary story, one that is true."

"I don't think he has to worry about sleeping through the night now," Lorraine put in.

"Oh," I said. "Is Kitty cured of her fears?

"Ah, no. She called this morning to invite us to another dinner party."

Detective Ingram sat up in his chair. "Oh, no."

"Yes, I'm afraid so."

I too was surprised. "So soon?"

"That's the reason she called," Lorraine went on. "She wants to have the dinner party in two weeks and was wondering if that was enough time to wait." Lorraine put on a Southern accent. "Out of respect for… you know, what happened. After all, she wasn't family."

I marveled at how quickly some people picked up the pieces of their normal lives with only a passing thought to a recent trauma. But this wasn't the time to dwell on human nature. I said, with an awkward, lighthearted smile, "It's good to hear that things are getting back to normal for Kitty."

"For Kitty, yes, but not for Harold. She told me that with everything that came to light during the investigation—she couldn't bring herself to say anything specific—Harold is sleeping down the hall in a guest room, the same one that Dr. Greene used."

"Poetic justice?" asked Ingram.

Lorraine shrugged with a crooked smile.

The Chief raised his eyebrows. "I'm glad I'm not living in his shoes."

In a glance, the two men shared a silent thought. "For more reasons than one."

I was sure it had something to do with having a wife like Kitty. Which got me wondering, did Harold enjoy being henpecked? It was a common occurrence in front of their friends. Did he like being told what to think and do? Outwardly, it appeared he did, but he had a rebellious streak. He took a young woman out for drinks, bought her diamond jewelry and who knew what else, all without his wife knowing a thing. Had he rebelled at other times in their marriage? If he was unhappy with the way Kitty treated him, why did he stay? Maybe she had the money that enabled them to build a custom home on the Shore and have lavish dinners? Sometime I'd have to ask Lorraine.

We enjoyed our little breakfast treats in quiet comfort which I soon interrupted with a question. "Oh, did you ever figure out what I saw in the woods, that red something?"

"I'm glad you reminded me," Ingram said after taking a sip of his coffee. "It was Dr. Greene's jacket."

"Wait," I turned to Lorraine for confirmation. "Wasn't he wearing a navy-blue sports jacket?" Lorraine nodded. "So, how—"

"After he killed Gretchen while wearing that jacket, he saw there was blood on his sleeves. At least there were wet spots that someone might notice. He took off his jacket, turned it inside out and you saw the bright red lining."

Lorraine made a face. "What well-dressed man has a jacket lined in bright red?"

Ingram shrugged. "Everyone has a secret side. Greene has a major one. Maybe the red lining was indicative of it." He reached for another donut. "I really shouldn't, but these donuts are delicious."

"Thank you. I'll pass along your comment to Mrs. Clark." Lorraine sounded grateful for the compliment and the return to a safe, unemotional topic.

"I have a question, detective. How did you know that the blood on the cufflinks matched Gretchen's blood?"

He gave me a tight smile. "I didn't. There wasn't time to do an analysis. I took a chance. It paid off. The lab has had time to confirm it is a match. It was you who closed the case, Abby. You found the cufflink. Somehow, everyone else missed it."

I shrugged a little as if it were nothing, but I was secretly thrilled that I could help.

After everyone left, Lorraine and I went outside to play with the dogs. In between throwing the balls for our Labs, who never seemed to tire of the game, we talked.

"You have been quiet about your impression and, I guess you could call it intuition about Dr. Greene," Lorraine said, avoiding my eyes. "I appreciate that."

All three dogs came crashing back and dropped their balls at our feet. Obediently, we launched them as far as we could, though I thought Lorraine was cheating. She had that pliable plastic hurler that sent a ball flying much farther than I could ever match. I made the silent promise to myself *again* to buy one at the local pet store to save my shoulder.

During the next respite, she continued. "I know you didn't like him… right from the beginning."

"No, I—"

I stopped when I saw she was shaking her head. "We've been through a lot together in a short amount of time. Give me a little credit for being able to read you."

Feeling self-conscious, I rubbed at an invisible dirty spot on my hand.

"I appreciate your caring. I hope you know that." I gave her a quick nod. "I know you were trying to do a little matchmaking and he might have been a catch… for someone else. I've been a widow for a long time and I'm comfortable. I'll never say I'll never fall in love again, but it's not a high priority. There is one thing I know. I don't ever want to have coffee and dessert with a killer ever again."

The thought of sitting on the Adirondack chairs enjoying the sunset with Dr. Greene sent a chill through me.

Lorraine adjusted herself so she faced me head on. "I want you to promise that you'll say something if you think I'm being silly or making a mistake. Be kind," she added with a smile, "but say something." She turned toward me. "You're becoming a good friend, Abby."

I smiled. "Yes, you are, Lorraine."

We laughed and headed back to the main house with the dogs scampering around us, ready for their treats.

ACKNOWLEDGEMENTS & NOTES

THANK YOU, READERS! Your excitement for this series makes it a joy to come up with another story for you. I hope you enjoy it.

Thank you to my beta and ARC readers. Your attention to detail and your encouragement helped make this book possible.

A special thank you to my dear writer friends Jen Peters and Donna K. Weaver. Your patience and support, especially when the finger was pointing, makes a huge difference in my life.

Funny names: There is a beautiful plant often seen on the Eastern Shore called Crepe Myrtle, because the delicate flowers resemble crepe paper: If you travel the United States and even around the world, you will encounter different names and spellings.

The scientific name is lagerstroemia crape myrtle. The traditional Southern spelling is "Crepe Myrtle." Across the U.S., it is more commonly known as "Crape Myrtle." In Europe and Australia, the scientific name Lagerstroemia Crape Myrtle is often used. Wikipedia insists that the correct spelling is Crape-myrtle.

Many universities that post articles about the plant refer to it as Crape Myrtle.

So, when you see the plant referenced in this story, don't jump to the conclusion that it's a typo. I opted to use the local spelling for the breathtaking plant that now towers over my house with delicate, showy pink flowers.

Susan Reiss
Saint Michaels, Maryland

October 2020

FIRST BOOK

When software developer Abby Strickland receives an unexpected inheritance sterling silver, her world turns upside down. The police arrive when her special cake server becomes a murder weapon. With blood on the family silver, she sets out to find the real killer. Lured to the crime scene in Saint Michaels, a sailing destination on the Chesapeake Bay, Abby finds a different way of life filled with quirky characters, boat races, a handsome guy.

And a tangled web of wealth, greed and family secrets.

SECOND BOOK

Sterling silver expert Abby Strickland wants to spend the holidays curled up with her books and her puppy, Simon. When an antique chalice disappears from a local church with a puzzle of clues left in its place, she is drawn into a dangerous treasure hunt.
Along the way, she learns about things that people do for love… and some they shouldn't.
Can she navigate the maze of secret desires
in time to save the spirit of the season…and a life?

THIRD BOOK

Accidental sleuth Abby Strickland goes to the Plein Air Art Festival where gifted artists compete for big prizes and fame. Elite art collectors eagerly search for their next acquisitions. Tension between rivals runs high as all are drawn into a net of creative envy, greed… and murder.

It's a charming summer event…
until somebody screams!

FOURTH BOOK

The discovery of an engraved bowl draws sterling silver expert Abby Strickland into a world where nothing is what it seems... where majestic sailboats unique to the Chesapeake Bay are called log canoes... hammered doesn't mean drunk... close friends become fierce competitors in the race for the coveted Governor's Cup Trophy.

Does the story of a century-old murder stay in the past or lead to blood and chaos in the water right in front of Abby's eyes? Was it an accident or was it revenge? Does the color purple lead to the killer or to a secret that puts Abby in danger?

Saint Michaels Silver Mysteries

FIFTH BOOK

The murder happens right in front of her eyes, yet Abby Strickland, silver expert and amateur sleuth, can't believe it! Was her dear friend Lorraine driven by jealousy to fire the shot or was someone lurking in the shadows?

A storm of suspicion and fraud upends her world of elegance as Mother Nature sends a deadly storm toward the Shore and Abby discovers she is surrounded by killers.